PANIC

COLIN SPENCER was born in London in 1933 and attended Brighton
Grammar School and Brighton Art College. From an early age, he was
interested in both art and writing and had his first stories published in *The
London Magazine* and *Encounter* when he was 22.

Spencer's first novel, *An Absurd Affair*, was published in 1961, but it
was with his second, *Anarchists in Love* (1963), the first in the four-volume
Generation sequence, that he began to garner widespread critical attention. Seven more novels followed between 1966 and 1978, including
Poppy, Mandragora and the New Sex (1966), *Asylum* (1966), and *Panic* (1971),
books that one critic has said 'revel in the eccentric, the bizarre, and the
grotesque'.

A man of many talents, Spencer is also a prolific author of non-fiction
books, including gay-interest titles like *Homosexuality: A History* (1995) and
The Gay Kama Sutra (1997) and acclaimed works on food and cooking
which led Germaine Greer to call him 'the greatest living food writer'.

More recently, Spencer has devoted himself to painting and to writing
a trilogy of autobiographical works, the first of which, the memoir
Backing into Light: My Father's Son, was published by Quartet in 2013. He
lives in East Sussex.

NOVELS BY COLIN SPENCER

COLIN SPENCER

PANIC

WITH A NEW INTRODUCTION BY THE AUTHOR

VALANCOURT BOOKS

Panic by Colin Spencer
First published London: Secker and Warburg, 1971
First Valancourt Books edition 2014
Reprinted from the 1972 Panther edition

Published by Valancourt Books, Richmond, Virginia
Publisher & Editor: JAMES D. JENKINS
20th Century Series Editor: SIMON STERN, University of Toronto
http://www.valancourtbooks.com

All Valancourt Books publications are printed on acid free paper
that meets all ANSI standards for archival quality paper.

ISBN 978-1-941147-03-0 (*trade paperback*)
Also available as an electronic book.

Set in Dante MT 11/13.2
Cover by M. S. Corley

INTRODUCTION

Murder is embedded in our culture, it lies at the heart. The domestic murder is perhaps the one that most fascinates and revolts us: as Cain and Abel and Greek drama illustrate, fratricide and all family killings are particularly repugnant. We propagate, we kill, the ecstasy of the former and the horror of the latter illustrate the continual struggle between death and life.

The thriller in its form, whether a novel, play or film, is a method by which we examine and interpret this nightmare. I had touched on the theme in other books but never placed it at the centre; what is more I took the very worst type of a murder to use, that of an infant girl: killing a child is the most monstrous of all slaughter, and to be near such an event is to suffer nightmares of the child's last moments. But there was a reason for this.

The emotional heart of the story stemmed from my own battle for proper access to my son in a divorce case, hence I felt bereft of the child I loved; creating Rod, his confusion and search was one way to deal with my own suffering. This was coupled with the need to shed some light on pederasts, for we should always fight against the lynch mob within society whenever it appears. If the lynch mob ethos becomes a fixed guiding principle in society's moral armoury it gains respectability and thus is dangerously acceptable. This, it seems to me, is what has happened in the forty years since the book was written, we loathe pederasts instead of attempting to understand them as emotionally stunted individuals whose sexual awakening was halted at an early age, believing always in the possibility that they can be cured of the affliction.

I have always loved Brighton; it appears in several of my novels, for it has an energy and an open, generous liberality, it embraces the kinky, the unconventional, the souls that never fit in. I discovered the Beach Bar in the fifties and used it as a setting for my first play, *The Ballad of the False Barman*, it harboured colourful eccentrics, full of cheap booze, misery and frenetic gaiety. I made friends with some and got to know their stories, I recognise now some of them in these pages. The main bookshop in Brighton at that time refused to stock my novels because they shed the wrong light on the town. Of course, they never took the same stand over Graham Greene and the petty criminal world he had painted, but then Greeneland was never sexually perverse and my novels when they depicted such characters and their environs gloried in it all and celebrated the oddness. Then, unlike now, it still had to be partially hidden, for most of the action in the book homosexuality was illegal and even when it became legal there was still so much guilt, humiliation and distaste that people like Trigger clung to the shadows and were mostly only around throughout the night. Trigger modelled herself on replicating Marlon Brando's look in *The Wild One* and at a quick glance achieved it. Old actresses that mourn their youthful beauty, who had little talent, like Saffron, are, I fear, too hackneyed in their appearances in film and book, yet they exist in all their colourful decrepitude, but I deliberately made Saffron more of a monster than most, as I needed Woody to be loathsome but, I hoped, also infinitely pitiable.

I had long wanted to try and tell a story in the first person from the viewpoint of several characters; as a teenager I had been moved and impressed by Faulkner's *As I Lay Dying*, always the perfect model for such a technique. Like all methods it has its drawbacks as well as advantages: you are able to get completely inside each character and from there control the narrative, but you also have to take on their view of the world which can be thoroughly repugnant.

My title stems, as the word does, from the God Pan; violence so often erupts from this feeling of anxiety, unease, darkness and ignorance, whereby some thoughtless, frenzied action appears to be an answer. Trotter defends his small patch of garden as the French farmer did his strip of land when Sir Jack Drummond and his family were slaughtered in 1952. Saffron gloats at one point as she mentions a whole family slaughtered with an axe; the story lurked at the back of my mind. As it did with Orson Welles who began a documentary on the case which was never finished. Welles's private theory, told to Huw Wheldon (then editor of the Arts programme *Monitor* at the BBC), who passed it on to me, was that in a war-ravaged Europe, and especially in the thin soil of that part of Provence, the farmer was outraged at the Drummond trespass, for the struggle over territory (Plato pins it down as the cause of all war) has been a source of murder since farming began.

COLIN SPENCER

February 25, 2014

PANIC

Part One

Crime and Penance

Rod

The shop door opened. The glass beads that were hung across it jangled; a deader sound than usual, possibly because Miss Curtis that morning had hung a lace collar there. I could still hear her silly, bright, unashamed voice, excusing it: 'It's very saleable. It's very saleable, Mr. Johnson, especially with the younger genera-tion, nowadays.' Why did her tone deepen into sourness upon the word 'nowadays', as if she hated everyone beneath thirty?

'So, they're still in the window, sir?'

There was no need to turn round. I knew who it was. I nodded and stubbed out the cigarette. I could feel him standing there behind me, in his grubby suit smelling of beer and petrol fumes, his large body looking helpless, almost powerless in repose.

'What's the game, sir, if I might ask?'

I looked up and he smiled down at me. 'They're not for sale,' I said.

'You don't think he's going to come in here and ask you how much they are, do you?'

I stood up. 'Who can tell? Mad people do anything.'

'Killers of that sort don't, sir,' and without noticing it, he picked up a fan, opened it out, then shut it back again, his large hand looking absurd as it touched the article.

'Look, Jones, I know you know their habits, what kind of men they are, where and how they travel. I know your theories, but I don't happen to believe in them completely. Did you come in here to tell me anything in particular?'

He half-turned away, then pursed his lips, making a short, melancholic hiss, a maddening characteristic he had. Then, as he

3

stared out of the shop window to the sunlight outside, he said: 'It's been almost a year, hasn't it? If he was a day-tripper, *you* think he might come back?'

I watched him. I didn't move. I didn't want to say anything.

'Supposing, just supposing, sir, that the man in question came back here, to Brighton. Maybe this month. And because he knew this was the shop and you were the father . . . let's suppose that he walked down this street and glanced in the window . . .' He turned round and stared at me.

I had to whisper then: 'Yes?'

'D'you really think his expression would alter, would change very much, if and when he saw the shoes?'

'I don't know.'

'Suppose he did, what would you do then – that is if you just happened to be here, in the shop, looking out of the window? What would you do, sir?'

I paused. 'I don't know.'

'Ah,' he said. 'You wouldn't think of ringing us, I suppose?'

'I don't know.'

'Slim evidence, a change of expression. Well,' he said as he started to go out of the shop, 'try not to give the alarm too often in the next few months, eh?'

Miss Curtis was just coming back, her string bag bulging with shopping. Her eyes immediately took on that look of alarm and suspense when she saw the Inspector. He murmured 'Good morning' to her, and she hurried in to me, almost breathless. I ignored her questioning expression and pushed past her, going to the window and staring out at the Saturday morning crowds. I remembered that yesterday I had seen a man unwinding a bandage; he was standing in the street unwinding this long thin bandage, a look on his face of such concentrated intensity, yet the bandage was so ridiculously small.

The shop opposite that I had sold last year had five window-gazers lined along the pavement. The new owner, a Mrs. Wainwright, in her fifties, her face a mask of enamel paint, had crammed the interior with recent reproduction furniture and fittings of unbearable gloss and gilt; while the shop I stood in now had nothing better in it than junk. Previously I had used it for storage, filling it with cheaper – though originally good – furniture that a customer could buy and do up himself. Everything in it was broken or crumbling; for a year nothing had been added to it, and very little had been sold from it; and for most of this last winter it had been home. The debris, the miscellany of these faded and frail articles – the beads and broken clocks, the decorated glass lampshades, the china chamberpots, a black beaded dress, the cracked, riveted plates, bowls and cups, a stuffed owl, the god Pan and a bouquet of wax flowers – they all seemed in some odd way to cover my impoverishment; they surrounded me with a reflection of the despair I felt.

'Well?' Miss Curtis asked.

'Nothing, Miss Curtis, nothing,' I said, without looking at her, afraid to see that face like some mean predatory creature disappointed of its kill. 'As you're here, I'll go out and get some lunch.'

She said: 'Oh, but Mr. Johnson, I could easily make you . . .' But I had shut the door. I went to the corner tobacconist's. The two packages of twenty of the brand I smoked were laid upon the newspaper as they saw me enter.

'It looks as if we're in for some good weather now,' he said jovially. His moustache was cut thin, just above his upper lip in the style of a thirties film star. He was over sixty now, but he acted with florid gallantry to every young woman who entered the shop. His manner towards me in this last year had been painfully embarrassing, yet still I went into the shop. Nine months ago he was saying: 'So they still haven't found him yet? Tut, tut, what you must be feeling, Mr. Johnson. None of our children are safe nowadays, none of them.'

He hadn't any children of course. Probably impotent. Throughout the year he went on making comments, informing other customers who I was; yet still I went in there everyday for those cigarettes, when there were other tobacconists just as near.

I smiled and took up the packets. I crossed North Street, running out behind a bus – a car hooted angrily – and ran into the beginning of The Lanes. I suppose I didn't want the crime to be forgotten. I went in there, to that shop, so that I could go on hearing him talking, however crassly; so that I knew it was still upon some people's minds. But this summer there had been another murder. A woman serving in an off licence had been battered to death. The police hadn't found the killer; nor would they, people said. It was the trippers. It was never, never anyone who lived in the town; oh no, everything unpleasant and shameful was blamed on those who lived elsewhere.

I walked across The Lanes and into Ship Street. It was the first hot day of this summer. The beaches would be crowded; the youths lying supine over the pebbles, strumming their guitars; their girls curled up beside them. Short, stout Jewesses, stalking in their white peep-toed shoes upon the pink pavements, arm-in-arm with identical friends, wearing, with pomp and pride, their fur stoles. Old men in braces, their wives unrolling their lisle stockings, peeling them from celery-white legs. Sailors from Portsmouth sitting outside the beach pubs, drinking pints of innocuous-tasting beer and wiping their mouths on their sleeves. And children . . . children everywhere, girls of six like Lucy, holding aloft tiny multicoloured plastic windmills, or licking mounds of ice cream with slow and avid delight; children laughing, skipping, shouting; children crawling, running, swinging; children paddling and splashing; and somewhere, somewhere among them all, a man . . . a man who watches their games. Who will look different. *He must look different.*

A motor-boat curled across the blue expanse of sea from Palace Pier. The Guinness sign in the old fish-market struck one o'clock. A child screamed with fear as the seal ran out from the castle; the father laughed, but held her tight to him. The pebbles were brown and old with filth where the sea never washed them. A boat was being painted white. A waste-bin, disguised as a painted man with a yawning mouth, lay on its side. 'Vandals,' a woman said as I passed it. 'It's them again.'

Vandals? But it wasn't vandals that murdered my child; it wasn't they who snatched her away, who kept her for three days, and then left her in a stream below the Downs.

I stopped. I had been going to see Jumbo, my dwarf. At this time of day I always went to see him. But what was the use? Seeing Jones in the shop had disturbed me; the way they looked at you was unnerving, almost as if you were under suspicion yourself.

No, I turned to the left; I pushed through the crowds. A young woman, dressed in an absurd fashion and obviously from some beastly newspaper, had stopped a middle-aged couple; the woman held on to her hat and beamed, giggled and smiled, as if it were the most precious moment of her life.

I sat in the bar at the end of the pier and saw for a moment the reflection of myself in the bar mirror. Is that why Jones looked at me so? I was not yet forty, but I looked more. I was unshaven, balding, my cheekbones prominent and hard; the trousers I wore were far too big, held up by an old necktie; my green check shirt was torn; I wore sandals and no socks. The effect was not that of an enterprising antique-dealer, but more that of a drunk, a beach-comber . . . a man defeated, and with little hope. I grasped the glass with both hands and drank from it. And it wasn't – I saw this clearly – just last year; it wasn't the marriage, the tragedy of a child-murder, so much as . . . one's whole life: did I *need* to be a victim?

After the sordid event is over, after the newspapers, the murmurs and whispers of neighbours as one walks down the street; after the identification of the tiny corpse, after the sleeping pills, the drink and the drugs; one is suddenly alone. It is as if a giant hand has torn a gaping hole in the fabric of one's life, and at last, for the first time, you stare through the hole and look. Alone, cold and naked, shivering and trembling, you go on looking, because you *have* to go on looking; it is impossible to turn away from seeing the motives of your life, the cowardly rejections, the helpless panic negations; to see how you failed. And yet you go on living, even if now you know that living means failure.

'. . . I told Bill, if you think I'm going to stay here alone, you're mistaken,' the barmaid said, a fat fifty-year-old. Her bulging breasts settled comfortably upon the bar counter as she leant over and spoke to a customer, who had worn today – obviously to celebrate the June sun – a vaguely nautical costume. 'Them ruffians just come in and knock you off,' she said vigorously. 'And when you're perched out here on top of a wave, who's to hear you if you do scream?'

'It's a terrible lot they are. It's a terrible lot they are,' the nautical man intoned mournfully.

'They don't think nothing of just battering your head in for a few coppers. What I'd like to know is what kind of homes they come from. Why, when I was young . . .'

I moved away. I took the glass and moved down the side of the bar and stared out at the window. A girl nodded through the glass and waved at me. I turned away and sat down. I hadn't recognized her; maybe she had mistaken me for someone else.

The motor-boat engine roared, then gradually died away in the distance. A man was shouting about prizes in a lucky dip; we had to guess how many people go on the pier this year. 'All for a good cause. All for a good cause,' he shouted. Sounds merged into one another: ghost trains clattered; arrows from bows hissed; metal racehorses clacked along tracks; elephants gave threepenny rides, waving their trunks up and down. The smell of recently-caught fish and salt water; the smell of sea-food and jacket potatoes. Three youths in black leather tried their strength; two of them roared at the other with scorn as the needle moved only modestly. I walked away from them, down through the crowds, past all the absurd little stalls selling mounds of gaudy and useless gimmicks.

Then a touch on my arm, and the voice: light and without anxiety. 'You didn't recognize me, did you?'

I turned. It was the girl. Of course, I knew her now. She had visited us several times two years ago. She was some distant relation of my wife's family; I couldn't remember what. Then she had gone abroad. Where? I couldn't remember; some travelling scholarship to do research. To America perhaps?

She leant over the balustrade of the pier. 'I see you've sold the shop. What a pity.' I looked away from her, down to the sea below; I knew she would ask the question soon, because of course she wouldn't have known what had happened; not if she had only just come back. And suddenly, desperately, I wanted to be with someone who didn't know. . . . I wanted freedom, just for a few minutes.

A pink scarf about her neck flew out in the slight breeze and framed her blonde hair and one sun-tanned cheek, as she said: 'And how's your wife? And Lucy?'

I answered too quickly, too lightly perhaps; but I couldn't look at her as I said it. I looked away, down to the swirling colours of the sea. 'They've gone away,' I said. 'Gone away, forever.'

There was a pause; then she said she was sorry. I could have mapped out every word and every sentence that she was going to say. 'But you do see Lucy? You were so fond of her. She was such a lovely little girl. She had such a tremendous sense of fun and gaiety.'

Was this the kind of punishment I'd asked for? Could I go on hearing what she said? I nodded. 'Yes, she loved dancing too. The last time I saw her she was going to her dancing class.' I spoke slowly. I half-turned away from the sea and looked at the girl, and then away past her, to the strolling couples, the sleeping fathers snoring their midday away in striped deckchairs. 'I saw her,' I repeated.

'You've got thinner,' she said slowly. 'In fact, you don't look at all well.'

'I saw her turn the end of the road, and four days later I saw her again.'

'Yes?' she said. 'Yes?' frowning a little, suddenly rather nervous, her slender fingers tying and retying the knot of the scarf.

'Dead,' I said. 'The dancing shoes tied tightly about her neck. Another pair, exactly similar, are in the shop window now. Exhibit A.'

I pushed away from her. She had made a short, sudden sound of surprise and horror, and now I was crying. I hadn't cried for almost a year. But I walked down the pier and stared at their feet, everyone's absurdly silly feet, and thought of her white satin shoes and the way they danced and moved across the polished floor – the sapele wood of the living-room.

I caught a bus. I sat on the top deck in the front as the bus moved slowly up St. James's Street. I thought of the house, the house that I was going back to. For the whole of the winter it had been up for sale; then suddenly I stopped wanting to sell it. It was the last thing I had of her; how could I let it go so easily? The furniture had been sold and stacked; the curtains had been taken down; but there were some broken toys in her cupboard, and her drawings of the ginger cat next door pinned up on her bedroom wall.

I got off the bus at College Street and walked round the corner. The house was white with a dark blue front door. Newspapers fluttered about over the steps; an empty tea packet, a piece of orange peel. The clay pots that held last year's geraniums had been cracked by frost; the stems of the flowers were black. The house inside was silent. It had always been a quiet house, but now the emptiness and the silence seemed to come together to fuse into some heavy, unseen substance, and opening a door and going into a room was cutting the substance, cleaving it apart.

What was the girl's name? Why hadn't I just told her what had happened? Or else just avoided her, said I'd never seen her before? Why the hell had I made such a fool of myself, running away, crying? Was it that I wanted her sympathy? I could see her, sitting here in this house with a book on her knee, the sun shining across her body in a bar of sudden white light, and my wife, my wife saying . . . 'Rod never reads poetry now; in fact, he never seems to read anything.' What a strange and pointless lie that was. I knew it for a lie then, yet I never bothered to correct it. I stood there, by the book-shelves, now all empty, and remembered that I'd looked away, embarrassed by what she had said. Perhaps she had thought the girl – Emma, was that her name? – to be some sort of rival. She was always frightened of other women. Or perhaps she wanted to seem more cultured?

I went into our bedroom. Some of her clothes were still hanging in one of the fitted cupboards: a check maternity dress, a fawn coat, two summer dresses, a pair of shoes. I took out the maternity dress and held it out in front of me.

I wanted to light a fire and burn everything.

Don't go into Lucy's room. I want to go into her bedroom. I want to be there again. I want to open the cupboard she used to store her toys in. *Don't, don't,* the voice still says, and yet here I am, in the room, and I am feeling nothing. Nothing. I feel released. I can look round the room, staring at everything that's still left here. There – d'you see her drawings? That's the marmalade cat, with whiskers as long as telegraph poles, and ears as sharp as wolves'; and over there pinned to the wall is the painting of an angel, and a robot, and . . . what was the other thing? I stare at it. There are three daubed figures, smudged in their bright green, blue and saffron-yellow on the biscuit-coloured paper; I can see the angel, for those are wings, and the robot – he has a tiny head – but the other figure – what is that? I close my eyes and try to remember her voice. 'Daddy,' she said, 'I've just painted an angel and a robot and a . . .' Oh God, what was it? I stare at it again. Was it some horned creature? I stare at it with intensity, as if it contained the whole mystery of her death. 'What name did she call you?' I whisper. And then I feel it, the pain, so vast, so dry and brittle, beginning to break and churn within my chest. I turn away. I needn't open her cupboard; no, there's no need. I know why I've gone back, why I had to go into her room: maybe I was afraid I had stopped feeling. No, it wasn't just that. The third figure, the mystery figure, Lucy's killer; I can't rest, I can't rest until I know who it is and why he did it.

I go to the top room, an L-shaped room, both study and living-room; there used to be a piano here and a record player. Lucy would march and dance to *Peter and the Wolf* . . . sometimes she'd sing the parts too; she'd sing them out loud and clear, her oval pointed face lifted up towards the ceiling. There is nothing in the room now, except some broken banisters; the dust lies every-where; the dark green walls are smudged and lined where pictures once hung. Were we ever happy in this house? I thought so once, but I can hardly believe it now; all I can recall is quarrelling, bitter recriminations . . . and Josie's face – which seemed so young, so pretty – distorted by suffering.

Miss Curtis said: 'I've just made a cup of tea. Would you like one? You look tired. Why don't you sit down?'

I took the tea and looked up at her. I was sitting at the back of the shop behind a desk, still piled high with books and magazines that needed sorting. I wondered why she always wore a grey dress. 'How is your father?' I murmured.

She flushed a little, pleased that I had bothered to ask. 'Oh, as well as can be expected, Mr. Johnson. He's past eighty, you know.'

I knew too well. She never tired of informing me of his age, his moods, his appetite and his illnesses.

'But his eyesight is still good,' she added, 'and that's a great blessing. Though of course he only bothers to read the papers now.' She took up some plates and began to wipe them. Suddenly I wanted to offend her, to splinter that eggshell reserve, to prise open her dusty mediocrity.

'Why do you always look at me like that?' I shouted.

She jumped. 'Pardon, Mr. Johnson?'

'You look at me with a mixture of distaste and pity. D'you know I despise your pity, I abhor and loathe your pity . . .'

'Well, really, Mr. Johnson,' she said nervously, and started to pile the plates up one upon another.

'You think I've let myself go; that's the vulgar middle-class phrase, isn't it? That I can't get over my grief. That I live off it. That I go around looking like a tramp, that I drink too much and never eat . . .'

I stood up and came round the other side of the desk. 'Do you know what my lunch was today? Four bottles of Guinness.'

She was beginning to cry. Why the hell did she have to cry? I wanted her to shout back at me. 'Well, really, Mr. Johnson, you're quite wrong, you really are . . .' she managed to sob.

'For God's sake, what the hell do you understand? You sidle in here every morning with your grey face and your grey dress, take your felt hat off, pin your hair in place, and all the time you're staring half at me. What are you hoping for? Another vulgar tragedy? D'you think I'll shoot my brains out? Or gas myself? Is that what you're waiting for? . . .'

She looked up at me, then fumbled for a handkerchief, and finding it she wiped her eyes, not with the customary genteel dabbing, but savagely, as if now she despised herself for such a feminine weakness. The words came uneasily; she paused between them, trying to get her breath. . . . 'I can't help . . . feeling for you. I'm . . . sorry.' Then with a moment's pride: 'Really sorry, if what I feel offends you. But there it is.'

I looked away from her. She had shamed me.

'Pardon my asking, Mr. Johnson,' she went on, 'but . . . but . . .' she swallowed, 'You used to have friends. What's happened to them now?'

'I embarrass them,' I said, and drank the tea.

'What's up then, Roddy?' His strange husky voice sounded sad, really sad. 'I haven't seen you for three days.'

'Let me help,' I said, and took the glasses from him and began to stack them on the counter. He ran away across the bar, clearing the tables, but looking round at me every now and again to see that I was still there. The bar was upon the beach, and the sun was low over the sea.

Mrs. Shirley Wilson looked hard at the sailor and said: 'Feel my breasts. Now guess – how old d'you think I am?'

It's like horses' teeth, I thought, and turned away; but I could still see them in the mirror. The sailor's loose mouth in its wide-open hungry grin, his fleshy hands pressing down over the cog marks in her thin blouse. 'I bet you're not more'n forty,' he said in a slurred voice.

She pushed his hands back upon the counter. 'I'm a grand-mother, you know;' she stated the fact with unctuous relish. 'And I'm forty-seven this Tuesday.'

The dwarf had me by the hand. 'I'll see you in the corner in five minutes, Roddy.' I nodded, then off he ran again. His twin brother had died a few years ago; they'd done an act for forty years in a circus. Now he eked out a living in this sordid dump. I had drifted close to him ever since *it* had happened; his vulnerability comforted me. Perhaps I still had to father something, however grotesque? One evening he had pointed out to me his hideout, near the bar, beneath the Esplanade, a small crescent-shaped attic used years ago as a storeroom and now forgotten. Jumbo was proud of it. He'd begun to show it to me, we'd gone up some broken back stairs and reached a loft door, then he paused and looked thoughtful.

'No, Roddy, I can't.' He shook his head, then clutched my arm fondly. 'I'm never alone there. I have friends. But . . . they wouldn't trust me again if I took you up.' He wouldn't say any more. I didn't ask. Jumbo often had an air of theatrical secrecy about him.

'No. You're not kidding,' the sailor was saying, rolling his eyes, his hands edging up to her breasts again.

Mrs. Wilson drew her lace bolero over her plunging neckline and leant over the bar. 'Ain't that so, 'Ilda,' she said. 'This gentle-man doesn't believe my age.'

Hilda drew a pint, her grey hair flying up around her wizened face. 'You believe anything she says, sonny. Shirley Wilson's a respectable woman,' and she turned away from them, her expression as immovably sour as it always was.

Cilia Black curdled her low notes on some ballad of lost love from the juke-box; a young negress in a flame-silk dress, her skin the colour of coffee beans, danced alone. 'A barley wine for Jumbo,' I said, and took that and my whisky to the corner. He was already there, lost on the huge and crumbling bus seat. By precedence and long custom it belonged to Big Lulu, but she hadn't come in yet. She ruled and mothered all the female tarts in Brighton, and most evenings she worked from here. She would take over the double bus seat – it had been patched and darned in several places, but still the stuffing frothed from it in places like yellow lather – as if it were her throne, while Jumbo hurried to bring her port and brandy. When she wasn't there, it was his mischievousness that made him sit upon it.

He drew his short stout legs up beneath him and sipped greed-ily at the strong beer, then he nodded for me to sit by him. 'I've been waiting for you to come in, Roddy,' he said excitedly. 'Trigger said she's remembered something.'

'What?' I asked wearily.

He leant his grotesque clown's face near to mine. 'She won't say,' he whispered, 'not to me, she won't. But she'll be in here later. She'll tell you then.'

I put my head in my hands. 'Jumbo,' I whispered, 'I'm so tired and so lost.'

'That reminds me,' he said cheerfully, 'when Jolly and me, we ran away from the circus. They were treating us so badly'; he said the word 'badly' with a long, low, musical sigh. The Animals were singing now, and more girls were dancing.

'Yes, Jumbo,' I nodded. But I was thinking of all the times in this last year when I had come here to this bar and heard their whispered information, and paid money for an address, a name, a street. For there was no sexual deviation that this bar was not aware of; and I was past caring if they told me lies, past caring that they partly lived off me, for that was their life; and this pursuit, this search, was *my* life now.

Jumbo went on talking, and the sound of his voice, which spanned two octaves in his excitement, fused with the jukebox, the sound of the girls' high heels clicking upon the concrete floor, and the shrieks, chatter and drunken laughter of the customers.

I remembered how, this last year, I would drive Jumbo to some

slum children's playground, the square asphalt bordered by thin
scaly winter trees; and there we would wait to the sound of a foot-
ball thumping against a wall. Jumbo would define with insensate
gusto different methods of indecent exposure, and we would wait,
and go on waiting, driving back there or to some other equally
depressing place another day. Sometimes thin and seedy men
would be pointed out to me. I got to know the way they stare at
children. I would get out of the car and go across the road and lean
on the railings near them, staring hard into their faces. All I saw
was hunger. Then, sometimes, they would look at me with a look
of conspiracy, as if to say; 'D'you love them like that, too?' They
terrified me; their obsession was so immovable, so much the entire
flame in their whole existence, that it would drive me back into
the car, shaking and trembling. Starlit Joe only exposes himself
at dusk in the winter, while Ted the Snatcher pinches little girls'
underclothes from washing lines; little Mr. Pond has a weakness
for always giving them toffee apples first; and snowy-haired Bill
Drake, with the meek face of a saint, has been in and out of prison
all his life. The list went on; the permutations of their fulfilments
were endless; the sordid nonsensical details of their drab lives
began to build up a commonplace web that only saddened me.
For how could I believe these men, so weak, so inadequate, had
anything to do with murder? Yet I went to the police, every week,
and sometimes every day of every week; I began to drive Jones
mad. He knew all of them. The information that I had carefully
sought and paid for he already knew in the utmost detail.

'You must understand, sir,' Jones said, 'that most of these men
are weak in the head. None of them can even begin to drive a
car. And we know that the body was brought there at night and
dumped by a car. Now, these men, if they did do anything violent,
they'd panic at once, and they'd be discovered in a matter of hours.
You're wasting your time, Mr. Johnson. Can't you see that, sir?' He
paused, and added sourly: 'And my time, too, I might say.'

I knew his theories, I knew them backwards; I was sick of hearing him, with his large stubby fingers tapping the desk, saying: 'It
bears all the hallmarks of other cases along the south coast in the
last ten years. The dancing shoes prove it. I have compared notes
of cases in Bognor, Bournemouth and Eastbourne. . . .'

'When was the case in Bournemouth?'

'That was the first, a girl of eight going to her dancing class, her shoes tied . . .'

'I know. And the Bognor one?'

'Two years later. And the case at Eastbourne eighteen months after that. The girl there wasn't quite dead; but she died before regaining consciousness.'

'Brighton lies between Bognor and Eastbourne; isn't it likely that he lives in this town?'

Jones shrugged.

'Were they . . . all of them, like Lucy?'

'Much the same, much the same, Mr. Johnson,' he said briskly.

'Yes, but . . . how, exactly?'

He looked at me with eyes that were suddenly tired. 'Dance frocks all missing, either bound up in a sack or wrapped in a bit of blanket, traces of barbiturates found in all the bodies.'

'Heavy doses?'

'Fairly . . . that's something to be relieved about, sir, don't suppose they knew much of what was happening.'

'They'd be unconscious?'

'Almost certainly, sir.'

'But . . .'

'Look, Mr. Johnson, we are doing everything we can. You know that. Go home and leave it to us.'

Go home and leave it to us. And now, here was the girl they called Trigger, dressed in jeans and black leather, her golden curls cut short and close to her head. She whispered: 'I dun' wan' Jumbo to 'ear, an' it'll cost yer a fiver, okay?'

I gave her the money, bought her a whisky, and she drew me away through the crowds to the bench beneath the window. She is lesbian and often mistaken for a man; her profile is almost Roman and is handsome; but her hands are small and fleshy, as pink as an expensive doll's. She edged near me and smiled. One of her front teeth was broken; it was black and jagged like a criminal instrument. 'Me an' me mate,' she whispered, 'we did the clubs last summer, see. Well, we did 'em all, all over the south coast.' The

words 'south coast' reminded me of Jones and his theory. 'We did
well, too. Three 'undred nicker a week. Not bad, eh?'

'Not bad,' I echoed.

'We didn't touch many in Brighton. Too dangerous. They know
me 'ere, you see.'

I swilled the whisky around in my glass, looking at her with
a curious fascination. I remembered that they called her Trigger
because she'd shot at a policeman when she was fifteen and had
gone to Holloway for five years. I prepared myself to hear another
story made up of lies, half-lies and resentful accusations against
some persons who had offended her. She looked away, through
to the dancers. 'I'm a bloody fool,' she muttered, 'three 'undred
bloody nicker and I go spend it all on me girl.'

'Go on. What were you going to tell me?'

'Off she flies to Paris, spends it on dresses at Dior an' perfume,
and all that kind of lark.' Then she added: 'And she didn't stay
with me more'n three months. I don't think she was really bent,
y'see, Roddy, not really. An' they used to call her Duchess in prison
because of the airs she gave 'erself.' She looked remote, almost
beautiful, her skin a pale gold merging into the deeper bronze of
her hair. Then she turned and looked at me. 'Why d'you want to
find this bloke, then?'

I paused for a moment, then I murmured: 'It's none of your
business.'

She said at once: 'Yes, it is, 'cause I think I know 'oo it is. An' if I
tell you where to find 'im . . . well . . .' she drank her whisky down
in one gulp.

'How can you possibly know?' I said sharply.

She didn't say anything; she sat there, then nodded at her glass.
I went to the bar and bought two more drinks. The negress had
been joined by two others and Beth, a plump lesbian with badly
dyed hair, who used to go around with Sadie, Trigger's new girl.
They were all dancing together, their black shiny arms entwined in
each other, their small breasts pressed tightly together. They made
Beth look even uglier than usual. Suddenly I felt lust; I wanted to
drag one away – the young negress in the flame-coloured dress,
her hair tinted red – drag her away from the other lesbians, down
on to the beach, to strip her naked and to make furious, helpless

love to her. I swore at Hilda: 'The bloody glasses are filthy. Can't you wash them?'

She sneered. 'Scram if you don't like slumming,' she muttered.

The whole bar seemed like some antechamber to hell. Why, I thought, they call it love . . . do they? All of them? And I watched the negress and she was beautiful; God, she was so beautiful. Her face had a spiritual intensity, a fire within it, and her body was like a burning liquid. . . . Your perversions are no better than what happened to my child. It's all the same; it's filthy, it's evil, and it ends in destruction and loathing.

I slammed the drink down in front of Trigger. 'I want her,' I said and nodded at the girl dancing.

'We all want 'er,' she said stonily. 'But she's married to the little fat one, and she'll knife yer if you as much as look at 'er girl.'

'Suppose I pay Big Lulu?'

'Are you crazy?' she said. 'What's got into you, Roddy? I thought you wanted to 'ear what I got to tell you . . .'

I turned away from the dancers. 'Go on,' and I looked out at the sea. The sun had gone down. The sea was partly silver, reflecting the gorgeous, crazy ebullience of the pier's lights. The scene looked unreal, like a carousel in a distorting mirror.

Trigger's voice was low. 'We raided this club in Brighton. We got into the office, but there wasn't a safe. I learnt afterwards that the bastard kept the safe in his private flat. But there was a desk, see, and the middle drawer was locked, so we broke it open, see . . . and what d'you think it was full of.'

I shook my head. I had begun to tremble. I was afraid.

'Big coloured glossy photographs of girls, most of them undressed, real dirty they were. . . . My God, he must 'ave been a filthy swine, close-ups, you know, of their quims and all. . . .'

'Shut up.' I was drunk. I couldn't think. The questions I asked her all ran into one. 'The club? Where is it? What's his name? Tell me, please. . . .'

She put her hand on my arm and whispered the name. 'Keep yer 'air on, Roddy, I'll take you there tonight, if you wanna go. . . . He's a rum bastard; he's got this big fat wife. Maybe it's 'er what collects 'em I mean, you can't tell.'

I drove Trigger along King's Road and up into Kemp Town. She

complained that my ancient Ford was filthy and uncomfortable. I
said politely that I hoped I wasn't putting her to too much trouble.
But it seemed that Sadie was waiting for her at the club.

I parked the car where she told me; then I said: 'Look, suppose,
just suppose, it is the man: he'll recognize me. He's sure to know
who I am from the damned pictures they took of me in the gutter
press.'

She shook her head. 'Just you wait, it's so filthy dark in there no
one can see yer. An' anyway, it wouldn't matter if 'e did; give 'im
a shock, wouldn't it?'

We went down some stone steps into a basement; there was a
striped plastic awning over a door, and beyond that a heavy baize
curtain. Inside, soft music, dull lights and a roulette table. Trigger
signed me in with a false name and kissed Sadie on the cheek. She
gave me a limp hand and smiled wanly. She looked like a painted
doll, her hair swept up into a massive beehive; she wore white plastic
daisies for earrings, and had a diminutively pretty, well made-up face.

Her thinness, her slightness, reminded me of Josie; I saw her
bony nakedness and felt again a surge of desire. Oh hell, I thought,
what made you turn into a hunted woman, someone who couldn't
rest until you had exploited every feeling I had for you?

'That's 'is wife,' Trigger murmured. I walked across to the
bar and bought them their drinks. The barmaid was a Jewess of
extraordinary ugliness, grotesquely fat; her black hair was piled
up in thick folds upon her head; there was a mole on her chin that
sprouted hairs. She served me without interest, though she could
see my face clearly in the light from the bar.

I took the drinks back to them. Trigger was watching the roulette wheel spin. Sadie turned her head and said with a strong
cockney accent: 'D'you think I look pretty tonight? Eh? Basil at the
West End Bar says I look like a film star. Guess which one?'

I murmured something and walked away back into the darkness of the club. 'Audrey Hepburn,' she called after me perkily.
I stumbled over somebody's feet and a man swore. There were
two of them in a chair, embracing. It was all wrong; I knew in my
bones that it was all wrong. It wouldn't have been anything to do
with this place.

It was late at night. There was a wind from the east that had swept the sea up over the promenade. Even here, beyond North Street, you could smell and taste the salt spray in the wind. Jumbo sat wrapped in a rug in the room at the back of the shop where my bed was; he sat on the floor nursing a bottle of whisky, framed by all the junk and litter that could not be crammed into the main part of the shop.

It didn't seem to me in the least absurd that he was the only person I now could talk to or confide in; if he by heredity was an outcast, I was too, through accident. And yet – was it accident? – this problem obsessed me. Night and day I would try to analyse what in my life had caused it; surely there was a reason why I or my wife had not been at that moment with Lucy, a time of two minutes. Those two minutes seemed like naked stones rolling backwards and forwards upon an arid desert. Those two minutes were the tear in the cloth through which every notion and belief I once held had been sucked into nothing.

'We were quarrelling,' I said. 'I watched Lucy walk down the road; I watched her from the shop door. I was shouting at Josie – I can't for the life of me remember what about now. I watched her turn the corner. Five yards, that's all; five yards down that street was the house of her friend. She was to ring the bell, she was to ring it as she had done every Wednesday for a year, and the friend was waiting to take her to the dancing class, a short bus-ride away. And yet, she never got there. The friend was ill, the mother was waiting to send Lucy back, but they discovered afterwards that the bell was out of order. And yet in those five yards, and in that space of two or three minutes, she disappeared.'

Jumbo sighed. 'Can't you remember what you were quarrelling about?'

'Does it matter?' But I knew he was right in an odd way; it did matter. Everything mattered that comprised the moment of loss. I saw a tear begin to form upon the dwarf's lower lid; it swelled like a sphere of glass and ran down his cheek.

'To love is a terrible thing,' he murmured. 'It feeds upon us like a parasite. We get locked in its embrace and can't ever find the way out.' He paused and looked up at me with a strange, deflated, twisted air, as if he knew he'd come to the end of all pretence and had to say the words that would force me out. 'And was it she, the little girl, your child,' he said, 'the only creature in God's world you ever loved?'

He saw me nod and take the whisky, pouring it into a tumbler and drinking from it, as if that burning liquid could stop the fact that one abhorred most.

'Why be ashamed?' he went on. 'To love one thing is something in this miserable goddamned world. At least you've come out the right side, holding half an angel's wing. Think of Lulu, the great slob, she'll go down beneath the earth sinking back into her mound of flesh without having once glanced away from it.'

'Don't you see?' I cried, and I slipped from off the bed and on to the floor, going across the floor and appealing to him, or trying to, in my half-crazed, half-drunken way. 'I could love only the child in my whole life. My parents were okay, they did what they felt was necessary for their children, but . . . there was no warmth, no feeling, or if there was they never showed it. Oh, perfectly respectable people living shallow, smug lives, content to accept everything second-hand. I didn't even love my mistress, and she was a late development. She got so sick and tired of embracing a carcass, a framework of flesh and bone, that only thought it loved, that only thought it felt, that she had to go, leave, come back again, make anguished requests from me; for I didn't understand what was wrong, nor did she. And so I get married. I'm thirty-three. But the mistress goes on writing anguished letters. I burn them. I think Josie never knows. But of course she does, women know everything. They know it, they smell it, they taste it. Josie felt she was sold down the line, so the kid gets born. And that poor helpless little human being is loved by both of us so hugely, so possessively. Then comes the moment when we each realize that we don't love each other, but only the child.'

I stopped. I'd forgotten what I was trying to say. I was trying to explain my pain to him, but even now I was bewildered at the cause of it. 'At first, I felt . . . yes,' I went on, 'that we deserved to lose her. But why should she deserve that end? She was innocent, innocent of everything. But that's what Josie felt, she must have felt that. She couldn't endure to stay with me. She had to go back home, to her parents. And then after we knew, she lay there, in bed, for days and weeks; just there in bed, saying nothing. She couldn't eat or drink, she wouldn't. She wouldn't live at all, and when at last her mother said: "She wants to see you, to talk to you, there's something, something else that's bothering her," I drove over. I went up into the bedroom, and she was dead. She'd called me over, then she'd taken the pills, because she had to say, to explain in that way *only*, that she had to give me this great big nothing, this huge faceless monster that she'd been living with. And then, and then . . . the parents. Jack, my father-in-law, limped about the cottage, suddenly moving furniture, as if their only daughter's suicide necessitated rearranging material objects to cover the loss. And Nora, the mother, she looked at me through her fingers, covering her face. They both stared at me as if I had caused it all. And in a sense I had . . . caused it by not being, caused it by not loving, caused it by neglect, negation.'

His tiny hands gripped my fingers. 'And why must you find him? Why that?'

'To understand. That's all, I want to understand him. If he's caused this. . . . No, he caused nothing, he just took away what I loved. The only thing I ever loved . . . then I must find out, I must understand why he did it. What secret pattern led him to my child? What was the path he took? Who were his parents, guardians? How has he loved and not loved. And what torment makes him destroy innocence and purity? I must know!' I shouted, holding on to the dwarf's arms and shaking him.

His great face, yellow and tanned by age and the weather, looked up at mine, and his fingers held on to my jacket and he shook his head, slowly, backwards and forwards, and his tiny bright eyes looked blind, unseeing. 'It can't help,' he screeched out like an old parrot. 'It can't help you at all. The ones that destroy, their hopelessness is deeper, emptier than yours. . . .'

'I must see him. I must see his face. I must look into his eyes.' I shook the dwarf's coat as I said the words, and he seemed to grow smaller, as if now I was frightening him. Then I stopped. The silence suddenly seemed limitless.

'And will you take a knife to him?' he whispered.

I lay down on the floor, my head was in his lap. He began to stroke my hair, tenderly, softly, his coarse hands as gentle as a woman's.

'I want to know,' I said, 'that's all. I don't want to punish him, to judge him. But I have to see if I can feel compassion for him, and I can only loathe and hate him if I don't understand why and how he could do it. There's nothing violent here, except this nausea, this sickness I feel for myself, locked away, imprisoned by my ignorance. At first, you see, he was a devil, a cruel maniac. When you started to take me through the streets of the town, through to the places where I'd never been and never thought existed, and began to show me who and what they were. . . . How could I hate them? How could I even judge their inadequate, ashamed desires? I could see them too clearly, and how they were lost too. How they had been trying, all their childhood, and all their life since then, to find something for a moment, or a half-moment, to care for, for some other human object to admire them for one second. . . .'

I closed my eyes.

He said: 'In Europe, in the war, we were put in a cage, like animals. For a time I crawled about the cage, round it and round it, knocking my head against the walls, corners, doors, bars. They laughed, they just laughed, Roddy. Dwarfs are very funny, you see, when they behave like tigers.'

Jones didn't even bother to look up. He sat behind the desk, reading, or pretending to. 'Well?' he murmured.

'I rang you three times yesterday, and twice this morning.'

He sighed. 'Yes, they told me. What do you want?' He lifted his mottled face and stared at me, then taking an empty matchbox, he broke it in his hand.

I moved the few steps towards his desk and looked down at him. His eyes were dull and red-rimmed. He glanced away and opened a drawer, then tore off a piece of the matchbox, and still looking down at the interior of the drawer, he began to pick his teeth with it.

'Did you always drink as much as this?' he murmured in the same uninterested, rather disconsolate, tone. 'You reek of it. It can't be doing you much good.'

I told him the name of the club. I told him the name of the

owner and that I had had information about the contents of a locked drawer in the office of the club. He turned the chair round and stared down at the low windows. The Mayor's car was being parked outside. A policeman opened the door of the office and laid a file down on the desk.

Jones moved the file and said: 'Thank you.'

The policeman went out of the office and shut the door quietly. Jones began to go through the file, taking out a paper, and with a short pencil, scribbling words in the margin. Then he said: 'Did you hear me, sir? I said "thank you".'

I might have turned and walked away without another word. I almost did. But the feeling of his disinterest, the abstract way that he represented the justice we so clumsily searched for – and perhaps too, the wind rattling the window at that moment and sending a sudden squall of rain against it – pricked my desolation, so that I had to say, had to go on: 'Just for once,' I shouted, 'admit that you didn't know it. Admit that this particular man at this particular address, having a particular obsession that may or may not be abnormal, harmful, cruel, or even, let me say it, against the law . . . admit that you were ignorant of all this.'

He looked up at me and sucked in his lips, then said with a certain crude triumph: 'Your young friend . . . no doubt she forgot to tell you that she'd stolen the photographs, and that she's been selling them ever since. The models were not juveniles.' He stood up. 'And when you see her next, sir, just tell her from me to try and go straight. We've got her partner on another job, but one false move of hers and she's back inside.'

'That man, what about him?' I said sullenly.

'Last summer, when the crime was committed, he was ill in hospital, seriously ill. And besides, he's not the type; he just likes women.'

I nodded. Then as I was opening the door to leave, he said: 'And, sir, do you have to go to that bar? Why don't you leave the town? Pull up your roots and go to London. In time we'll get the man, I promise you.'

I crossed the car-park and went into the Star and Garter. It was almost empty. I drank a pint of beer slowly. What roots? I thought. I haven't got any, and that was the trouble. How could my parents, now retired in their bungalow at Peacehaven – reading the *Telegraph*, walking the dogs, looking at television – have given me anything durable and illuminating? I closed my eyes and remembered that I had sworn to myself that Lucy would have in her childhood what I had never found. And yet in giving her love, we lost it all for each other. When Josie was dead, I could not even feel sorrow. I stared down at the bed, at the coffin, at the grave; I stared at it, and somewhere within me there was relief, but not sorrow. And I was relieved because I knew what hell it would have been for us both to have gone on seeing the other, and knowing how we had failed, and what inadvertently we had caused.

A slim hand placed a drink down upon the beer barrel next to me. She said: 'D'you mind? I'll go away if you want me to, but I had to say how sorry . . .' The voice trailed off. I looked up and saw the girl, the girl from the pier.

'It's Emma, isn't it?' Her long hair was brushed back from her face; her features were sharp and bony. She was embarrassed now, and nervous; her words, which I hardly attended to, were rushed and jagged. 'Can you forgive me?' she ended up by saying, and I laughed.

'For God's sake, what the hell is there for me to forgive? I behaved badly, foolishly; I didn't want to talk to you. I don't want to talk to you now.'

She got up, but I grabbed her hand and pulled her back down. 'You see, I don't talk sense, I don't talk any sense. I didn't mean that. Or rather, I did, in a way. I don't want to talk, but I want you here. . . .'

Emma looked at me curiously, frowning slightly. 'Why don't you just sell up the other shop and go away?' she said.

I was staring at her, wondering if all I wanted was just to go to bed with her, to undress her, to unpeel that pale pink dress, to draw it away from her shoulders. Would her nakedness tell me anything I didn't know already?

'Why did Josie resent you so?' she said.

'I disappointed her. She resented her own hopes of what marriage might have been, and as she couldn't take it out on her own illusions, she took it out on me. Have you got a lover?' I asked.

Emma shrugged. 'In the States, maybe, but it won't work. He's the type that goes to bed just to pin another scalp on his belt; it becomes a bore.' She bent down over her glass, and I could see the slender curve of her neck; how frail it looked. I tried to imagine her in bed. She had inside her vulnerability a hardness; she could live off resentment too. Like Josie, I thought.

'Please . . . if there's anything I can do, anything at all . . .' Her sweetness was in her eyes; they were dark blue, given depth and feeling by the tawny gold of her hair. She had said those words before, her fingers playing with the glass. I wanted to hold her to me, to clutch at her body, to grasp at her clothes, to feel her face next to mine. But I knew what I felt had nothing or little to do with sex. It certainly wasn't love. It was desperation, a pleading and begging . . . for human warmth and consolation. Yes, but also to pass through that, to try to find something tough and ugly; the grief in her, so that mine would not exist alone.

'In Los Angeles I went to bed with a man, and I stayed there with him for a week,' she said in a tired child's voice. 'He tried so hard to love me. Each bout of sexual activity seemed to him proof. But it proved nothing to me, nothing at all. I used to lie there naked, just covered with a sheet, and observe him. I knew every gesture he'd make, I knew every square inch of his naked body . . . my knowledge of his body was so complete, maybe that's enough? That's all we have in the end, isn't it?' She paused, and then added: 'We lived off popcorn for two days. D'you know, there was nothing, just nothing at all, that man could do except sex. He couldn't sing or anything. He never sang a note, in all that week. You'd think a man who's naked and walking around a room for seven days would sing sometimes, wouldn't you?'

She finished her drink, then turned towards me, still with that air of astonishment, but this time waiting. It was as if in the two years since I had last seen her, she had tried to become a woman, and now she was amazed and troubled because she had failed. 'I've got the car outside,' I said. 'Shall we drive out of the town?' She said nothing, but stood up. Her hands were flat upon her thighs, and I could see for a moment the shape of her body beneath the thin dress.

I knew I drove badly. I drove fast, I took risks, I braked suddenly and turned corners sharply, I hooted angrily at other drivers.

Emma sat there in the seat moving with the car, her thin arm held out straight before her to steady her body as it moved and jolted, her face expressionless, her look completely unenquiring. I turned inland behind Newhaven, and she got out of the car. Without saying anything, she began to pick twigs and foliage, straggling with the thicker branches and tearing the bark in white strips from the trees. The leaves were still wet with the recent rain and her dress was marked. She threw down what she had collected by the side of the road, then turned to me and pointed. 'I'll race you, I will,' she shouted, 'to the top of the hill. Come along.'

I watched her. She turned to see what I was doing, and the wind caught at her hair so that it covered her face in a thick veil. I ran. Our two figures moved, zigzagging across the incline, the thick hummocky turf rolling away beneath us. Then the rain began to fall, softly, filling the air with a fine mist, and the pink glow of her dress in front of me was like a fruit, the last unpicked fruit in an orchard. I could hear her laughter inside the wind. And as we ran up towards the top of the hill, I could feel, rather than see, the way she moved, turning and twisting across the hill as if she were trying to find her way in a labyrinth of narrow streets, or as if it were a game, and she was trying to disguise her tracks. I stumbled and fell; there was a pain in my chest, but I went on running. And suddenly I knew it wasn't a game, that she was part of flight itself, and that her story of her seven days in the bedroom at Los Angeles was the story of another pursuit and flight, that she had insisted that they stay there, together in that one room, hoping by that act to stop the movement. But she couldn't, because there was a panic within her.

'I wanted to run on. To never stop. To go on and on. . . .'

We lay close together, out of breath, on top of the hill. 'Why?' She turned away from me and picked at the grass petulantly. The sun shone through the sea mist like yellow silk. 'Take me back now,' she whispered. 'I must change.'

'Where are you staying?'

'With my uncle, where I lived as a child.' Then she chanted: 'Mr. Norwood Willoughby, or Uncle Woody as they always call him. And Lord, how his name fits.'

'No parents?'

'What?'

We strolled lazily back down, then stopped beneath a straggly group of trees. 'What happened to your parents?' She began to whistle softly, a long note that grew louder, then she said: 'Bang. Puff of smoke.'

'Both of them?'

Emma nodded. 'Doodlebug, fell short, right on the square patch of lawn five houses down. Ours was sliced in two.' She shrugged. 'They were in the wrong half.'

'Where were you?'

'At a party. Never wanted to go either. Hated parties. But . . . my father, he was in the Navy, back on a short leave . . . daresay they wanted to be . . . well, alone.' She turned to me, smiling, but said resentfully: 'I can still remember begging my mother not to send me. I think . . . yes, sometimes I think that was the only thing she ever forced me to do.'

Emma picked up the foliage and threw it into the back of the car. As she got in, she said: 'Let's go down on the beach. I want to swim.'

'But it's still raining.'

She shook her head as if to say it was entirely irrelevant. I turned the car round.

We stepped across the rocks below Telscombe: limbless and headless torsos lying upon their sides. Pools of chalk draped with black seaweed, pony-grey pebbles as large and as oval as ostrich eggs. The sea shifted uneasily, rattling the smaller pebbles. The beach was empty.

We stood there, then she said: 'When I was very small, when they were still alive, I had a game I used to play.' She shivered. 'It was quite horrid.' Then she turned to me, her face so bright, alive and candid. 'I think I was a very good child, you know, obedient. Never gave trouble, no tantrums, withdrawn maybe. I suppose I felt so vulnerable that I couldn't risk enraging the world, in case they hurt me, but . . .'

'The game?'

'If the world did – other schoolgirls, mistresses, neighbours . . . all those kind of people – well, I would take their cruelty quite meekly, but then for days and weeks afterwards I'd lie awake and plan the most revolting revenges upon them, real Grimm fairy-tale punishments.'

I laughed. 'Why does that still seem to matter to you? You're not telling me they all turned into toads?'

She shook her head, still very serious. 'Oh no, nothing happened to them, nothing at all.' Then she took off her dress and stood there in her underclothes. The rain shone on her body. She kicked off her shoes, and bending her arms back, she unhooked the small white brassière that supported breasts of little weight but perfect roundness. I sat with my back against the cliff, smoking and watching her slow careful movements as she stepped out of the white knickers and kicked them onto her dress. Then she moved slowly, picking her way over the beach, down towards the sea. I called to her: 'Be careful, the rocks are sharp beneath the sea.' But she didn't pause, her long brown legs bending and moving on, supporting the straight tear-shaped torso. She walked on, bending down and holding on to the rocks and feeling her way round them; the sea reached her thighs and then her waist, and then she began to swim. The mist hung just above the sea and she merged into it.

Everything upon the beach below the mist shone with a translucent clarity, as if the scattered objects of the beach-scape had been outlined in luminous white. As I sat there among these broken bones of an eroding cliff, I longed to sink my consciousness back into *their* time . . . their faceted shape, their relationship to each other, their silence and stillness, the way they sprang from the beach like fossilized plants, their square roots buried in shingle; and I saw my anguish dwarfed by their wisdom.

Later that night in the bar I could not rid myself of the beach; as if the way it looked had been significantly planned, as if the beach itself contained a secret, and I was too obtuse to have found it. Against the raw wail of the juke-box the dwarf had taken Emma's hands and was dancing with her, dancing with great solemnity, lifting his short legs up gaily and stamping them down again; she moved, her head held high, circling slowly round him. They ignored the laughter from the bar.

'Jones is right,' I said, 'I've been behaving like an idiot. I must leave the town. I must get out of here, go away, leave England, go abroad, go anywhere. . . .'

Jumbo took a quick look at the girl and licked his lips, then he shrugged and laid his podgy hands upon the table. 'Wherever you go, you won't rest; you'll keep moving on. . . .'

'That's better than staying here, surely, and circling round and round on the same spot. Why shouldn't I move on? Why should I care that I hate this maniac who murdered my child? Why shouldn't I go on hating him? Why shouldn't I exult when they catch him and lock him up for the rest of his days?'

'You're obsessed about justice,' Emma said, 'aren't you? Sometimes you pretend not to be, but you are. What the hell is really going on in your mind about that man? Don't you believe that society should be protected from him? Don't you believe that other people's children should be saved from him?'

'He thinks,' Jumbo said with a sly look, 'that there's such a thing as the hidden law, a secret justice, and that it has already worked upon him. And now poor Roddy commits himself to the punishment.'

The girl looked up; her hair, still damp, was tangled. She drew it back behind her ear, looked about the bar and murmured: 'I don't understand. I just don't understand.'

'You told me today,' I said quietly, 'that you had never forgotten the photographs of the bombed house of your childhood. That you were too small, too young, to remember the event, but that you had never forgotten seeing the photographs when you were a little older, how the house had been sliced in two, how it looked in all its detail. . . .'

She put her hand to her breast. 'It seemed to be myself,' she murmured.

'I thought that I couldn't rest until I knew who that man was. Parts of our awareness get trapped sometimes in objects and people that have a separate existence from ourselves. In your case, a photograph. In mine, that man.'

'How can you ever know him?' she said with scorn. 'How can you? If the police caught him, d'you think they'd even let you talk to him, see him alone?'

I drove her home past Seven Dials and turned off Dyke Road. 'I forget,' I said. 'How were you related to Josie?'

'My Uncle Woody married her aunt: Nora's sister. It didn't last for long. She divorced him.'

We reached the road, a narrow cul-de-sac. She turned to me: 'Please come in.'

I stopped the car. 'I'm no good in bed. I've tried . . . ever since . . . but . . .' She took my hand and laughed gently. 'I feel it all, yes, but the body . . . it's just dead.' She pressed my hand against her cheek.

I followed her into the house; it seemed huge and gloomy. We went into a drawing-room crammed with heavy Edwardian furniture. She poured me out a whisky, then stared at me. 'Horrid, isn't it? I hate this room and everything in it. Well, not quite'; she nodded at a large bookcase crammed with ornately bound volumes. 'When I was small, that saved me.' I noticed a cello in one corner and wondered whether anyone ever played it.

We heard a voice, frightened and querulous, calling: 'Emma? Emma, is that you?'

She went to the door and opened it. 'Of course it is. Come along down.' She turned to me and said softly: 'Be kind to him.'

'Are you alone?' her uncle asked. I could hear his footsteps in the hall.

'No, I'm with a friend.' She left the room and they appeared together, her arm entwined in his. 'Have you been out today?' He shook his head. 'But you've eaten, haven't you? You did eat what I left for you?' He nodded and peered into the room; his eyes were masked by thick spectacles. 'This is Rod, Uncle Woody.' She led him towards me. His handshake was limp, and I could see he had difficulty in focusing, because he stared at my face for some time, then mumbled a greeting. He felt for a chair and sat wearily down.

'I waited up for you. You know I always do that.'

'It's absurd,' Emma said. 'It's long past your bedtime.'

He shook his head and half-turned to me. 'I can't sleep. I never sleep. Wake up, you know, all hours. I worry.'

She laughed. 'Now about what? I've told you if you want a nurse here all the time, if that will make you feel any safer. . . .'

'No, just you. She's a good girl. She always was a good girl. But she ran away and never told us where she was. . . .' Uncle Woody

shook his head again sadly, and I saw that she became suddenly
tense. She rose, picked the whisky up and nodded to me.

'We're going upstairs, Uncle. You'll be all right, won't you?'

He didn't answer and we left the room. 'How bad is his eyesight?'

She led the way upstairs and opened the door of a room immediately above the one we'd left. 'Oh, he knows this house so well
that he could get around blind quite easily.'

She switched the light on, and I saw we were in a room so different from the rest of the house that I felt a momentary shock. It was
painted white and was almost bare of furniture; it was both study
and bedroom and ran the whole length of the house.

'This was her room, his mother's. Old Saffron May Willoughby,
what a horror she was.' Emma shivered slightly. 'After she'd gone
he sold everything in it, and what he couldn't sell he burnt.' She
smiled at me. 'He's still convinced it's full of ghosts.'

'Hers?'

'And others. He refuses ever to enter it. I'm not surprised. The
two of them always seemed to be in spiritual communication with
something or other.'

'He seems now . . . so pathetic.'

She sat down in a cane rocking-chair and moved it gently to and
fro. 'He clings on to me. . . .'

'That's obvious.'

She sipped at the whisky. 'I don't know why. Perhaps he thinks
I'm aware of something she knew.'

'What?'

'She used an odd kind of tyranny over him.' Then she shrugged.
'Perhaps it was nothing. A child sees all sorts of imaginary terrors
in quite natural situations.'

'Were you unhappy here?'

She paused, staring at me intently. 'I was never happy, but. . . .
No, I can't remember being actually miserable. The whole house
had a terrifying enchantment. I was constantly involved in it.'

I looked down at a long pine trestle-table, piled high with books,
and strewn with typewritten sheets. 'What are you working on?'

I had bent over the table and was beginning to read from one of
the corrected sheets. 'Please,' she said, 'it's nothing. I don't want
to talk about it.'

We heard his footsteps on the landing outside, and then the sound of a key in a door. 'He locks himself in.'

'Why is he so frightened?'

She didn't answer, but poured out more whisky for both of us. I remembered the name of the cul-de-sac, Monk's Lane, and something stirred in my memory. She crossed to the table and started to close the book and shuffle the papers into place. She sighed. 'Really, it's absurd. You might call it a Victorian Scandal about a mass butcher in the Colonies who was condoned by the society and the government of his time.' She raised her glass and murmured: 'The roots of violence.'

I took her gently in my arms and kissed her. Was it the word 'violence' that provoked such an unpremeditated gesture? Her soft lips were parted, and she slipped her tongue quickly into my mouth. I pressed her body hard to mine; I could taste the tang of whisky on our tongues. She seemed like any other woman: there was nothing tangible, definite and idiosyncratic about the feel of her flesh; yet there was a mystery about her that I longed to explore.

She broke away and sat down in the same chair, then she shook her head. 'Silly, really . . . I don't know why, but I still feel so ashamed of it.' She nodded over to the table covered in pages of the typescript. 'It's just that it goes back to my childhood, and that . . .' She broke off and stared about the room. 'There were so many mysteries, perhaps I thought . . . that this one . . . at least I could find out about . . .'

'The mass butcher?'

'My great-grandfather. Last year, I went to Barbados. The island that still loathes him.' She paused again, so far away in her thoughts I knew I couldn't reach her, then suddenly she said: 'D'you know, my father lived in this house as a child? And yet when I lived here, they were so secretive and twisted, they never actually told me that? And d'you know, he ran away too, like I did, only he ran away when he was fifteen, earlier, three years earlier than when I at last got away. And on Sundays there was this stupid Bible reading that old Saffron May would insist on. I had to stand in this room and read out passages from the Psalms, and . . . but she'd changed some of the words and they were all passages that had the word "Dove" in them.' She paused. 'It was horrid actually, quite horrid.'

'You hated it here. Why on earth did you come back?'

She twisted round in her chair and stared at me as if startled. Then she suddenly began to twist her fingers. 'I . . . I'm not sure. Perhaps there is something I have to find out. And . . . I'm all poor Woody's got. Just the two of us, that's all now that's left.'

She bewildered me. 'What, Emma? What is it you have to find out?'

She turned her face away. 'Don't ask me. Not yet. Please.'

I heard my voice murmur, 'It's no good, it's no good, no good at all.' We were lying naked in the dark, covered only by a sheet.

'What does that matter? We're here, warm and close to each other, that's all,' and she nibbled my ear. 'I like your arms. I feel safe in them.' Then she whispered: 'You remember the game . . . that one I used to play as a child? You remember what I told you on the beach?'

'Yes. Yes.'

There was a long pause. I could feel her body next to mine, tense, as if all the nerves were concentrated in a hard knot. 'Well . . . when it happened, when they – my parents – were blown to bits . . . you know what I thought?'

'What?'

'That I'd caused it. Don't you see? – by my wickedness. That was the way I was punished. . . .'

'Emma, dear Emma,' I whispered.

'It's not absurd, not for a child. . . . I was convinced . . . maybe I still am.'

We lay there in the dark in silence. I felt close, united, almost as if we were both concentrated in one human substance. But beneath that warm intimacy something else was disturbing me: those words she had used before: 'violence', 'scandal', 'terror'; they seemed to grow in my mind like a black fungus thrusting up from my unconscious. There was something too about the street and the house that united with them. She stretched out her arm, took a cigarette and lit it. The flame briefly glowed above her face; it was strangely impassive and withdrawn.

I sat up in bed. 'Something did happen here. I remember. It was this house.' I struggled to find the light, and when I switched it on I saw that she had turned and hidden her face in the pillow. 'What was it?' I shook her.

'Please,' she murmured, 'please.' She stubbed out the cigarette, then turned her face towards me and tried to say one word.

'What?' and I shook her again.

'Murder,' she said.

I stared down at her in disbelief. The outrage of past violence uniting with my own confused anguish seemed a total mockery of the life we clung on to. Then she began to sob, and in her tears and hysteria, told me shattered parts of the horror, as if it had happened that same day. I held her close and tight in my arms as she shook with pain and revulsion, her body moving uncontrollably, reliving what she had seen as a girl of sixteen. Her nails clawed my back and thighs, my teeth bit into her neck and breasts; and as I saw, through her words, the final grotesque disgust of violent death, I felt swollen, huge and hard inside her.

Woody

I had been waiting for an hour or more, watching from an upstairs window for their arrival. I was thirteen and my mother had left to meet my father's ship at Portsmouth on his return from France; she had now been away a whole week, for they had gone to stay at our house in London. I had been told not to join them there when my term ended, but to come here to Abbot's Lodge where my father's old nanny lived in retirement. They had written to her yesterday and told her they would be down this weekend and to prepare three rooms. I was afraid my father must have been wounded far more severely than I had been told, for I could sense that something was strangely wrong.

The cab drew up into the drive and my father, resplendent in his major's uniform, his left arm in a sling, got out and paid the fare, fumbling with his one hand, then slowly my mother climbed down. I saw she was wearing a new hat and coat; a veil covered her face, and an ermine stole was tied neatly beneath her chin. Then she turned towards the inside of the cab and held up a small child. Beneath his cap he had fair hair and he clung to her tightly.

I left the room and stared down into the hall from the banisters. Nanny was laughing and kissing my father; then she picked up the boy and hugged him. I walked down the stairs; my mother raised her veil and kissed me on the cheek. I shook hands with my father.

He said: 'This is Thomas. He's going to live with us.' I turned to look at my mother; her face was bright and unconcerned, but I knew this particular expression: when embarrassed, the corners of her mouth would turn up in a semblance of a smile and her eyelids had a nervous flutter. She quickly unpeeled her gloves.

'He'd sure like some tea, Nanny,' she murmured, then she took my father's arm. 'We rode in the park, all yesterday, and my bones ache. I'm goin' to rest before dinner.'

Nanny held the child and chattered nonsense to him, and I thought of all the rejections I had suffered from them both so far, and that this intruder must be the ultimate one. But after that weekend, as if my parents felt a shred of guilt towards me, they took me to London with them, leaving the child in Nanny's care. They had rented a house in Sussex Gardens just north of the Park, and I spent the rest of my summer vacation there. The whole of London was in a state of frenzied excitement; the war had lasted for four years and everyone expected it to be over at any moment. Early in August, when the news came through that Haig had won a surprise attack near Amiens, people ran out into the streets shouting and cheering, certain that the Germans would beg for an armistice. My mother, always an excitable creature, was in a rage of activity; officers accompanied by exotically dressed women visited our house at all hours of the day and night; we seemed to be submerged in one continuous party. In the mornings when I entered the drawing-room downstairs, there were always strangers asleep on the sofas and in the chairs, and the rooms reeked of tobacco and spilt alcohol. Yet in all this gaiety and confusion I heard my parents quarrel as violently as they had always done. My father had suffered a shrapnel wound in his upper arm and though he would not be allowed to return to France he wanted to perform home duties at his own regimental base; as always, when he made a decision, he got his way, against every tantrum, ploy and artifice my mother used. At the beginning of September he left for Dorset, but the parties at the house continued, and now my mother was free to perform. My father hated her to sing or act in company; I think at these moments his jealousy would become almost uncontrollable, for at one afternoon soirée I had seen how when the guests begged her to sing, my father had quickly excused her, saying that she was suffering from a cold; she had laughingly denied that it was of any consequence, and had sung most readily *Daddy Wouldn't Buy me a Bow-wow.*

My father looked dour and fidgeted all through the song. At another time I overheard two of the guests mimicking my mother's accent and ridiculing her on some obscure point of manners. I learnt slowly that the truth was that as Sadie Stirling she had been accepted upon the London stage for her beauty and gaiety, but was known to be unreliable, for she drank more than was considered suitable. In their fierce quarrels, there were stock phrases that were screamed repeatedly; my mother claimed to possess a 'protector' – I had no idea what this meant, connecting it with Oliver Cromwell – but it appeared this 'protector' made her financially independent from any money my father had. How true this was I never finally found out, for my mother could never distinguish very clearly between what had happened and what she wished to have happened.

Neither did she have any sense of propriety, a constant source of disgust for me. In the morning she would drift about the house in a state of near nakedness and would spend hours in the day with oils, creams and sweetly smelling lotions, smoothing them slowly into her flesh with tiny circular motions of her fingers. She had no personal maid, claiming that she abhorred the presence of other women near, but used the housemaid to tend to her extensive wardrobe. Quite by accident I had seen her naked many times, and when I would hide my face or run from out of the room she would laugh; I think this natural reaction of mine deeply amused her, for she would go out of her way to taunt me.

The parties continued in my father's absence, but I noticed that most of the officers drifted away, and that now in their place more common soldiers appeared, and the songs that filled the house late at night were obscene trench songs, my mother's voice leading the choruses 'Mademoiselle d'Armentières, parlez-vous'; the gruff raucous sounds of the men drifting up to where I lay in bed, sleepless and tormented by her coldness towards me.

But one Welsh officer remained there every night; she referred to him as 'my sweet Davey'; he had a round podgy face, a wide smile, ginger whiskers, and a soft lazy voice; he walked stiffly about our house, for one of his kneecaps had been shot away, and neither of them ever disguised the fact that he shared her bed every night. She used to sing a popular French song of the time whenever he appeared; 'Je sais que vous êtes jolie.' He had a patient resignation about his manner, and loved to talk of Wales, where he had a farm of many acres, which included a ruined medieval castle. Once he began a mock wrestling match with me, and when I felt his hands upon me, I screamed and ran, for I had a morbid hatred of being touched. There had been an incident at my prep school when I had been ragged and set upon by the other boys; I kept a penknife in my pocket and had used it, stabbing it as deep and as forcefully as I could into their flesh. Their wounds had not been serious, but I had been brutally caned by the Headmaster, and because of my fierce refusal to return to that school, my father had sent me to a smaller establishment where my intense shyness and fear of physical bullying had so far been an armour against attack. I was alone, thought to be distinctly odd; my nose, even then, was over-long, and the frames of my spectacles for my short-sightedness had to be especially fitted, for my eyes were set close together. But I found that if I was obedient, neither slow nor too quick with my work, and never provoked the other boys, I could achieve a precarious security.

The war was still going well, people talked of the new machines called tanks, and of the steady influx of American soldiers who had been flooding into France for a year now. It was in the middle of September, and the following week I had to return to school; my mother told me that Father would be staying with us for a weekend before I left, but Davey was still in the house, and I was terrified of the quarrels that were certain to ensue. I spent the whole of Friday in the park; I had been given by Mother for my birthday a large grey battleship, and I spent hours floating it on Kensington Pond, but on Friday there was a steady downpour which began to stop only in the evening. I was alone in the rain at the pond, not caring that I was drenched, that my boots squelched and the rain ran down from my hair beneath my clothes. Any experience was better than what I would have to suffer if I returned to the house in Sussex Gardens, but the storm clouds encouraged the evening dusk and my own warm room seemed better than that sinister half-light. I trudged home and got into the house through the tradesmen's entrance in the basement. I was shivering with cold, but no one noticed me enter. I saw my father's suitcase still unpacked in the hall, but the house was oddly silent.

I took off my soaking wet clothes, dried myself and went to bed. Later I heard the door open, and my father came into the room. He saw the black puddle of damp on the carpet, the heap of clothes, said some angry words, came to my bed, and felt my brow and wrists. Then he quickly left the room, shouting. I was already beyond knowing exactly what he said, for I was exhausted with previous sleepless nights, the terror of his anticipated arrival, and the stony chill that seemed to have entered my bones. The house-maid lit a coal fire and brought some hot milk and brandy, which she forced down me, and which soon after I spewed up. I had a high fever, which turned soon afterwards into pneumonia; there was great talk of the influenza epidemic that was raging in Europe at the time, and I believe they thought I was going to die. I did not want to live, until I was suddenly aware that my mother was being kind to me. I had never known her as she was then, so gentle and sweet-natured; I had never before heard her voice pitched so softly, and the drawl of her accent was pure balm upon my wound of longing for her; even her clothes were dark and modestly deco-rated with the plainest jewellery. She waited on me. She read to me. But most of all I delighted in the way she told me of her own childhood. She sat in a wing-backed armchair, her hands clasped in her lap and stared away at nothing particular in the room, lost in the remembrance of those days, creating a vivid picture of total enchantment. The white house, its verandas and shutters, the near-tropical heat of Florida, the vast plantation, the happy negro workers picking cotton, the dappled pony and trap she was given on her eighth birthday, her white silk dresses and bonnets, her graceful dancing in the ballroom of the house which was the talk of the whole neighbourhood – for had not the world-famous actress Fanny Kemble come to the house herself and stayed there and watched Saffron May, the angel-child, and told my mother that one day she'd be an even greater actress than she was?

I did not know then that it was all lies, that my mother had never been to Florida in her life; that she had been born on the West Coast of vaudeville parents and endured as a child poverty and near-starvation.

Her myth excited and consoled me; if she had once known such happiness, then I might gain it too. Perhaps she could only show love to me through this myth, for it seemed to contain and strengthen us both. 'Sure I will,' she whispered, 'I'll take you back there, we'll spend a long summer's vacation. My, what a welcome we'll have, Woody. All the flags and bunting will be flying, and the town band playing, and the young beaus in their white suits doffing their hats to us as we ride down Main Street. They haven't forgotten me, I can tell you that, Woody. Why the Mayor will be there and there'll be feasts like you've never seen, suckling pigs and lobsters, pineapple puddings, syllabubs and ice cream.'

By the time the Armistice was finally signed, though still weak I was allowed up; the doctor told my mother that one lung had been damaged and I should not return to school for at least a year. This news gladdened me, and from then afterwards I took pains to increase my frailty by various tricks on the day of the doctor's visit. I would steal cigarettes from the drawing-room, and shutting myself in the lavatory with the window wide open, smoke ten or more one after the other; then going to my room, I would throw myself into wild energetic exercises, so that when the doctor arrived I would hardly be able to get my breath, it coming only in short hard gasps, choking and coughing.

It was only when I could get around the house that I realized nothing much had changed; the Armistice was an excuse for a mass of parties that continued for weeks, and though my father was often away, Davey was still living in the house and sharing my mother's bedroom. There was one strange significant difference, and that was that I never at the time heard them quarrel. My mother looked oddly triumphant; she always walked with a certain poise as if even material objects as she approached them would move away for her. But I felt now that the poise was more evident, that it had a sharp cutting edge upon it. Even the smallest routine gestures, like pulling on her suède gloves and adjusting her large osprey-adorned hats, were done with an element of tiny savagery, as if she were pursuing a secret revenge.

My father had always had a great love of classical music, and it was at this time that he acquired a cello and had twice-weekly lessons, coming home and practising in his study for long hours. He had a passion for Brahms. The clumsily executed phrases, played again and again with stubborn persistence, drove my mother out of the house. I believe this was his intention, for as soon as he heard the front door slam, and the absence of her voice, which was always loud and demanding, he would stop playing. Sometimes he would come and sit by me, and try, using his old school books, to teach me languages and mathematics. But I knew his mind was elsewhere; he always listened attentively for her return and would stop in the middle of some problem, walk to the window and stare out into the street, lost in thought. Though he was now discharged from the army, his absences from us grew longer, and when he returned he looked out of place, as if he could not convince himself that this was his home, my mother his wife, or I his only son. Was it weakness or strength that made him stay with us at all? For when my mother had tired of Davey, there were other lovers, though none that had the serene compliance to continue to live in the house when my father also inhabited it.

In the spring my mother had a sudden fierce infatuation for a young Lord – English titles fascinated her – and though he lacked all charm and physical attraction, she clung to him with an obsessive and ardent passion. At one time I saw her behave in such a menial way that I was sickened; she had herself polished his riding spurs, and I found her upon her knees in front of him fastening them on to his boots. Another day he had staggered out of the dining-room, blood streaming down the side of his face, screaming for help, and complaining that my mother had crushed a wine glass into his head. It was all the more bewildering when she appeared and with great composure took his hand and led him upstairs.

I think she really had some inane hopes of divorcing my father and marrying this man, for I overheard her murmuring his title one evening as she fastened the clasp of her pearls and stared into the mirror with a look of glowing admiration. But her basic crudity was always too strong for her to sustain a dignified role for long. The peer left the house for good, as so many of them did, with my mother, her clothes in disarray, screaming abuse and throwing anything near at hand at his departing figure. When he left she turned to me. She sat on the floor, her dark red hair uncoiled, weeping and lamenting, sipping at her glass of gin and water, and every now and again calling for my father: 'Where is he? Where is Francy?' she moaned.

Then she looked up at me with tear-stained appeal. 'Son, it's no good, son. He says we've gotta go, that there's no more damned money and . . .' she relapsed into her former weeping. 'If only that old witch, his mother, would die. What does she need all that money for? D'you know, Woody, he's too friggin' proud to go to her and ask. She loathes me. Well, how can she damn well tell, since she's never met me. So she is a general's widow . . . that don't mean nothin'.' She drew her shawl around her. 'I'm scared, son, I'll tell you plain. What are we goin' to do away from London?'

'Couldn't we go away?' I asked nervously.

She stared up at me furiously. 'Where the hell to?'

'Back to Florida, you said we would, wouldn't your family give us money?'

'Oh that,' she said disparagingly, then she gave a huge laugh. 'Goddamn me, that'd be the day.'

'Wouldn't they?'

She frowned at me. 'How do yuh think we'd get the fare, eh?' Then she moaned. 'I'm gettin' old, Woody, I don't look so good any more.' She paused. ''Course, if I had a play that had the right part. . . . Sadie Stirling as *The Second Mrs. Tanqueray*,' she sighed. 'Yeah, that might solve all our problems, eh?' She clutched her forehead with one hand. 'Okay, I couldn't remember the lines last time. Okay, I know that. But this time I'd make certain. I'd work hard at it, son, yeah . . . and then, why then, we could go to Florida like you say. They'd be proud to have us then. That's the time to go, not now.'

She struggled up and refilled her glass. She passed a mirror, momentarily posed in its reflection, then moaned and turned away. 'Who the hell is going to make us live in that dump?' she shouted. 'With his dirty little bastard crawling about the floor. Who the hell is goin' to make us, son?'

My father arrived within the month, and our trunks and suitcases were packed. My mother's mood had changed, and she greeted my father in a torment of longing, clutching on to his arm and covering his face with kisses, sighing and murmuring as she did so. They were oblivious of me, for my father's delight and ardour was as great as hers; I saw that he wept as he stroked her hair and kissed her lips repeatedly, and she seemed to be consumed by him. If he was not near enough for her to touch, she was in an immediate state of alarm and agitation. I began to understand why I had always felt so coldly rejected by them both: the frenzy of their feelings, that flamed now into love and then into hatred, excluded everything else except each other.

It was long before the war that my father had built Abbot's

Lodge, pulling down a house with the same name that stood on the site. He had built it and furnished it for my mother, but she had always refused to live there, a south coast sea resort being far too provincial for her taste; but my father had obstinately continued with his plan, buying up land and property around it, more as a debt of gratitude to his nanny, old Ada Trotter, who had spent her childhood in the cottage behind the house, than for any real liking for the town itself. For my father was not particularly conscious of the context in which he lived. While building this house, he had started an estate agency and bought other property, so that now he had a business that was fairly prosperous. He had more wealth than he ever allowed my mother to know, for she was stupidly extravagant, and unless we all lived modestly she would fall into her old *folie de grandeur* habits.

Ada loved the intruder, young Thomas, and made him her charge, and indulged the dribbling, simpering creature in all his treachery; she said quite boldly that he was the image of my father when he was the same age, while I obviously took after the old General's side. His widow did not take long to die, but my mother was bitterly disappointed over the results of her will. Her large fortune had been left in a trust to build schools, hospitals and dwellings for the negroes on the island of Barbados, in the understanding that such places were to be named in memory of her husband. My father heard some years later that the blacks were either too obstinately proud, or finally so stupid, that they refused to accept the munificence of my grandmother's gift, for the General's name was loathed with a depth and bitterness which only savages can feel.

When my father was at work, my mother gave strict instructions to Ada that she was not to see or hear the child; but on weekends, and when my father returned in the early evening, Thomas would be brought in to us and allowed to play. My mother then displayed a sweetness of temper and affection towards his continuous naughtiness, even to feeding him with her own hands, and generally created an atmosphere of patient love and restraint towards him.

Not only did we not benefit from my grandmother's fortune, but because of her death we were forced to feed and keep another person in the house: Bessie Wilkes, a pallid and dour spinster who had been in service in my grandmother's house ever since she was a small child. My father gave instructions that she was no longer a servant and must not be treated as such. But her nature was so feeble and the servile habit so strong in her, that she readily did whatever my mother or I told her to. As with Ada, my father was inclined to indulge her, and would always bring back small presents of chocolates and flowers for both of them, while entirely ignoring my own mother. He never seemed to notice that Wilkes was only embarrassed by these attentions, for all her life she had been both ignored and exploited and that was what her nature demanded. He even went so far as to encourage her in a silly infatuation for a violinist who played at the Grand Hotel. Wilkes entirely lost her reason and wrote the squalid little man love verses. My father bought her a fox fur and for one whole summer Wilkes mooned about the place, sighing and muttering to herself in an inane and distraught way. My mother in her scornful way told Wilkes that as a vaudeville Ophelia she would be a triumph.

I never returned to school; a tutor attended me, but as my eyes were weak and I complained bitterly that studying gave me severe headaches, my mother insisted that I was not to be overtaxed by unnecessary work. It was understood that eventually I would have a position in my father's business; this prospect was of no interest to me.

One day I found in one of the many old suitcases of my mother's a peg doll wearing a shred of clumsily sewn, bright hessian. This had an odd fascination for me, and I stole it and kept it hidden in my room. Secretly I made others, then I adapted them as puppets, and grew quite skilful in the making and manipulation of their limbs. My mother discovered this obsession, and to my surprise showed a quite excited delight, insisting that we must build a puppet theatre in one of the rooms in the attic, and that she would write plays and we'd both recite. For months we planned and built, keeping it all a secret from my father, who was told only that there was a surprise awaiting him in the attic. I remember this time so clearly, for it echoed the other time when I had been ill and she had shown such concern. We were both extraordinarily happy, and we got Wilkes to teach us how to sew and knit, though we were both clumsy, and it was Wilkes who finally made most of the costumes. My mother contented herself with the hats, which she cut out of felt and stuck with glue, then covered them with Christmas tree glitter and feathers from old pillows. It was my suggestion that the first play we performed might have some connection with my mother's happy Southern childhood. She liked this idea, but when she finally read the story out to me, it was about a cruel and vicious plantation owner, one Horatio Jagger, who burnt and murdered his slaves without just cause, and who only suffered a change of heart due to the pathetic pleading of his small daughter, Maisie, aged eight, who befriended, tended and secretly fed the poor slaves, and who threatened to throw herself into the fire if her father would not heed her cries for him to show the slaves mercy. My mother was very proud of this story, and would not hear a word of criticism from me that it lacked a clown, comedy or music. Finally she added a song to be sung by Maisie – that is herself – of happy jubilation to end the playlet.

We gave the play on Christmas Eve, and though Wilkes and Ada clapped heartily when we had finished, my father left the room immediately, complaining that it was all childishness. Later he called me into his study. I saw that he was very angry, though he attempted to control himself. He looked away. 'Norwood, I can see that I've foolishly neglected you. Since your illness you've done nothing but waste your time. Left to your own devices and hindered by your mother's foolish influence you've frittered away years which should have been spent in the acquisition of knowledge to fit you for the life to come. You are not a child any longer, and I will not have you behaving like one. All this will stop at once. On the first of January, you will begin work in my offices, and you will be treated like any other boy. You will be paid the same wage and put in the same hours. Is that understood?'

This new development irritated my mother, and flung us both into the roles of conspirators against the rest of the house. She began to drink now in the morning, and took a sudden delight in consuming huge amounts of food. She would hug me tightly to her and talk of Thomas. 'Blood will out,' was her favourite sinister comment. 'Born from a French poxy whore and behaves like a prince. We'll see, Woody, you and I, he'll suffer.'

She'd steal his toys and hide them; at other times she'd break them and leave them out, so that he would discover them destroyed and howl loudly. On Sunday mornings my father went riding upon the Downs; once when he was out she asked Nanny to bring Thomas into the drawing-room – he was about six at the time – she was pretending to write letters at her desk, but she played with the boy and encouraged him to draw for her with the pen she was using so that his fingers became ink-stained. She had already told me to go upstairs into his room and to pour ink over a new set of clothes. I was then to call the boy upstairs and leave him in his room. All this went according to plan, except that when Thomas was left in his room and saw the blue ink he let out a terrible wail, and hardly gave my mother time to complain to Nanny that a bottle of ink was missing from her desk. Nanny ran upstairs and scolded him for his naughtiness, and when my father returned and was told what had happened, we were both delighted to see him put the child across his knee and give him a thorough flogging with his belt. Nanny cried and begged my father to stop, so that she too was severely reprimanded for her over-indulgence towards the child.

Another time my mother scratched and gouged out the lettering engraved on a brass shield which was set into a huge turtle shell that hung in the hall. She did it very cleverly because she left the top line with my grandfather's name on it untouched as if Thomas had been too small to reach that far. This, too, worked successfully and Thomas was made to spend a whole day alone in his room. But our secret revenges eventually had to stop, for we both realized that Wilkes had been spying on us, and we feared she would inform my father. I deeply resented the fact that even though Thomas was so destructive and wilful, my father seemed to give him far more attention and love than I had ever received from him. In fact, for most of the time, my mother and I felt that in my father's eyes we hardly existed in the house. But our alliance with each other gave us great satisfaction.

My mother now took no interest in her appearance, and began to grow plump; I believe she was determined to destroy the physical attraction she once had, for it must have seemed her last and ultimate revenge upon my father. Her dark red hair lost its sheen, and she would wind it plainly into a knot at the nape of her neck; her breasts grew bulbous and sagged, and she purposely chose clothes that were either dull, or cheap and vulgar.

In the winter, while carrying two buckets of coal into the house, Ada foolishly slipped on an icy path, fell and broke her leg. She had to be taken to hospital and spend many months there while the bones mended. My father said she was too old to do the work that we expected of her, and Wilkes now took over all her duties, while my mother lay in bed until midday, reading cheap novels and eating sweets, claiming that nothing of interest ever happened and that she was fading away with unendurable boredom.

The office blunted my feelings; I did the tasks they set me to do, but I was treated by my father as a minor employee, even though I was now in my early twenties and other quite common men, only a little more experienced than I was, were preferred above me. I felt deeply the same sense of unspoken ridicule that I had endured at school. I was nervous and abnormally shy in the presence of young women, and sometimes, even walking down the street, turning towards Pavilion Gardens, I would feel myself sweat and my heart pound with fear if some young woman stared at me. In the particular branch office where I worked, there were two young secretaries, and often in the business of the day I would have to give them instructions. I preferred to do it by written notes, but sometimes because of their obtuseness they would not be clear upon some trivial matter, and would have to come into my small frosted-glass partitioned place to speak to me. I could not look at them. Their silly painted faces, all unmarked and as round and vacant as a rubber doll's, could put me in a terror of indecision, so that I would start to stutter. I hated the way they always tended themselves, like kittens, perpetually smoothing their stockings, powdering their faces and curling strands of hair around their fingers; but what appalled and embarrassed me most of all was my father's attitude to them; they seemed to bask in every word he said; his manner of assured gallantry with women they took as some overt sexual overture, and when he left their presence they would giggle and titter, wriggling upon their chairs with tiny movements of self-flattery.

Some relations of Ada's now came to live in the cottage to look after the old woman; she could only get about with difficulty and was more than useless; I believe it was her nephew and his wife; they had two small children whom we could hear playing in their back yard: a thickset tough little boy who stared at us all suspiciously, and a thin bony little wretch of a girl, called Alice, who had a pert little face and was impudent to everyone.

One Sunday morning, my father failed to return from riding. We waited; the Sunday dinner was spoilt, and eventually I was sent down to the stables to see if they knew where he was. Neither horse nor rider had returned, but by the time I had reached the house again, a policeman had already called and informed my mother of the news. She had collapsed in a storm of fury and tears, ministered to by a despairing Wilkes. Ada, though dry-eyed, was stubbornly silent, and it was some time before I could piece together what had happened. It seemed that upon the crest of one of the downs, the mare, a favourite creature of my father's but highly strung, had been frightened by the noise of a biplane that was out of control and which had swooped down over them both. She had bolted downhill; my father, though a cavalry officer, had failed to control the beast. Some peasants at Poynings had seen it all happen, and though they had run, being stiff-legged yokels, they had not been quick enough to impede her frantic progress, and she had charged into a thick copse which grew above the stream there; my father had been flung from his saddle, an oak branch had struck him senseless, and he had been dragged over the tangled roots. The mare had finally stopped in the stream. They found the body of my father half-submerged; he had drowned in a few inches of water.

He had always been a strong and healthy man, and I believe had thought he would far outlive my mother. He had made no will, and though my mother searched his desk, she found no written instructions providing for his bastard; indeed, if she had done she would have destroyed the document, but the lack of any intention, she told me, clearly guided her conscience in the matter. My mother inherited the whole estate, and we now saw new aspects of her character. At last in possession of no mean amount of money she came to a sense of purpose, vicious and self-indulgent as it was. Thomas was told to move from the house and into the Trotters' cottage with all his belongings; he had a fondness for making model aeroplanes and his room was crammed with these frail objects. Ada never recovered from the shock of my father's sudden death, and died a few weeks later. This death seemed to appal young Thomas, who was nearly fifteen then, and he became more than usually sullen and recalcitrant.

My mother went into deep mourning; she wore black for a year and would have nothing that belonged to my father removed from its place. I really believe her suffering was intense, but those depths of torment and desolation she now found within herself she explored, as was her nature, in the most theatrical and dramatic forms. She rightly appointed me as the manager of the estate agency, but made this announcement as a ceremonial, inviting the three senior members of the firm to the house. She had tinted her hair with henna and wore make-up of opaque whiteness; she sat in a high-backed chair in a long black lace dress, held an ebony stick in one hand and did not allow the three men to sit down.

'As all of you are so deeply aware,' she spoke slowly and softly, lingering upon each syllable as if the whole effort of creating words caused her pain, 'my late husband, Major Willoughby, was a rare gentleman of distinction with many generous qualities, a public-spirited man who, though not born or bred in this town, gave himself and the family fortune unstintingly to many respectable charities.' Then she jabbed the stick upon the floor. 'But what others did not know – how could they indeed? – was that no husband or father could have been so nobly loving, patient and gentle, that no family had such close-knit ties, such deep bonds of mutual affection, trust and love in each other.' She bravely dabbed her eyes with a black-bordered handkerchief. 'I have asked you here this afternoon to tell you that the brave tradition he represented will be carried on in the life of our two sons, Norwood and Thomas, though my younger son can fulfil no official duties, and it's my belief that his talents may lie in quite a different direction from those of his father.' She smiled sweetly and sighed. 'However, I know that you'll all be honoured to serve my eldest son and give him the respect and faithful service due to his name.'

Two of those three men resigned within the next six months,

but the third, George Pink, was more sly and devious; he wheedled his way, with an artful pretence of understanding and friendship, into a position of trust, so obliging and sympathetic to what I knew were my own shortcomings that for a period I relied upon him completely.

My father's death had disrupted the pattern of our relationships, so that suddenly we were all forced into different positions, having to observe new realities which rose out of the unknown confronting us with images difficult at first to recognize as ourselves. One summer evening, observing the smudged face of Alice through the conservatory stained glass, I realized my own nature. It came as an exalted revelation, but beneath that flood of feeling I was also aware that different shattered segments of my past had for the first time fitted together. But before that happened, Thomas ran away.

My mother's tempestuous fury at what she termed 'the brat's ingratitude' shocked me in its savagery. She broke up everything she could find in his room, and forbade us all ever to mention his name again. I think she needed him there to continue to humiliate; besides, he was part of my father, and she clung on to all the fading memories and images she had of him. But she made no move to find out where Thomas had gone, and it was years before we knew what had happened to him. Wilkes had kept her correspondence with the boy secret, fearing my mother's anger.

Yet there were times when my mother would be overcome with guilt over her past treatment of the boy, and she would cry and beg the shadows in her room that he would dutifully return, so that she could show him the kindness and love she claimed she had always felt for him. She started to go to spiritualist meetings, and though the services tended to bore her, she sat through those in order to join the séances. Then in Hove she discovered a medium, Mrs. Ethel Partridge, who she said enabled her to be in direct contact with my father. It was a great relief to her that he showed no anger or resentment at all over her treatment of Thomas, but informed her that the boy was happy and in a far-off place which had a sunny climate; that he, my father, now knew everything, and longed for my mother to have the same serenity; he said he was waiting for her, and through a spirit guide would always be near to her to help her in life's sorrow. Mrs. Partridge often came to the house, and on one occasion I was allowed to join them. After we had sat around the table, touching hands, and Mrs. Partridge had intoned soft words of command and contemplation, she slowly leant her head back, closed her eyes, and suddenly went quite rigid, so that both my hand and my mother's were pulled sharply forwards; then her body shook as if an electric current was passing through it. I saw my mother's face, which was charged with excitement; she stared with intensity in the dim light at the medium, whose throat I now saw was contracting, then expanding, but slowly like a flower upon the sea bed. She uttered no sound for some time, until the shaking subsided, then she spoke, but with the voice of a man, deep and rich, non-European sounds of torment, words that could have been protest, pain and tribulation – or just lunatic gobbledegook. The voice stopped as suddenly as it had begun. My mother looked disappointed, waiting for the medium to return to us. She surfaced slowly and with intense weariness, then she stared at us both with fear and shivered. 'Evil,' she murmured, 'evil, I've never felt it so strongly.' She stared about the room. 'It's not the house, the emanations don't come from the house.' She looked enquiringly at both of us. 'It's past and future, it's the timeless knot, Mrs. Willoughby, of violence that took me by the throat.'

'Oh dear,' my mother murmured, and she rose. 'Perhaps a tiny sherry?'

Mrs. Partridge shivered once more, violently, but the sherry seemed to dispel some of the gloom. I was not invited to join them in a séance again, and my mother grew secretive about further messages from the spirit world. She trusted the woman completely and relied on her with the faith of a child. But her relationship with Mrs. Partridge was terminated suddenly. She obtained a message from my father's spirit that Mrs. Partridge was to be given a large sum of money. It was the only message that my mother refused to believe was genuine; she returned to the house and claimed that her psychic powers were now as sensitive as Ethel's and that there was no need to rely on any intermediary between her and my father ever again. From then on she created her own séances, and though her trances never seemed to me as dramatically super-natural as Ethel's, my mother managed to enter that state with alarming ease, and always came out of it again with reassuring messages. But that was before 'it' happened. I refer to little Jenny Dove, and yes . . . oh yes, others. . . . Some, I never knew their names – their faces, yes, I can often remember – happy angels all of them, no doubt about that. Entrancing, as their tiny thumb and finger lifted their white flounced dresses, pirouetting in tiny white satin shoes. If only Alice had not encouraged me that first time, if only . . . I always knew it was wrong, but at the time it did not feel wrong, at the time it was right for me, right for them . . . there seemed no harm in it. Alice saw no harm. Alice liked what I did.

I had been half-dozing in the conservatory, and now I rose from the cane chair and saw her, crouched in our garden, her thin cotton dress bunched up about her waist; the fact that she used our garden like a stray cat to pee in possibly showed her disdain for us all, for she was a haughty minx. I watched, and slowly became immensely aware that my body was transformed by a hot river of excitement that quivered in the centre of me. Alice rose, tossed her hair back, and I found that without thinking of what I was doing, I was coming out into the garden, was smiling and chatting to her. She stared up at me suspiciously, fearing a reprimand. I found myself talking to her quite naturally about a flood of childish interests, then took her into the house and offered her the prettiest biscuits and cakes I could find; she ate them all wolfishly, spraying the table with crumbs, and I had been drawing closer to her all the time, and now had my arm around her tiny waist.

'Would you like to sit on my lap, Alice?'

She looked at me, grinned, then climbed down from the chair and on to my lap. I knew she wore no knickers.

'That's better, isn't it, Alice? You're a good girl, Alice, aren't you?' My hand was between her thin thighs, my fingers just tenderly stroking those fresh, plump lips. She grinned and tossed her hair and swayed a little. I felt no fear that Wilkes or my mother might enter the kitchen and discover us; in fact the thought never once entered my head. It was all over in a second. I felt the release of the discharge inside my trousers. I felt spent, happy, more deeply fulfilled than I'd ever known. I gave her half a crown which she inspected with delight, then she ran back through the garden. I did not even feel any anxiety that she would tell her parents what had happened; it all seemed so harmless, and how could she know anything of the ecstasy it gave me? But at the age of seven, Alice was far from innocent; her instinct was accurate: I knew it in the way she looked at me. She knew she had a strange power over me, that I would in fact have done anything to enjoy that pleasure again and again. I now secretly stocked the kitchen with little cakes and sweets that I thought she would enjoy. Always exactly the same thing happened; I had only to hold her on my lap, to touch her nakedness for a moment, and it was all over. Of course in time my mother grew aware that I was friendly with Alice, and it puzzled her; here was something she could not begin to understand, and she had always felt that she had complete comprehension over me. My delight in this secret joy gave me strength against her constant demands for attention; doing what I did seemed in some odd way to crush her. So perhaps it was not a physical delight, but some devious way my imagination worked whereby I felt that at last I had power over her.

But I grew bold and careless; not only did we do it in the kitchen, but also in the garden, any place where I would suddenly come across those sweet secret charms of Alice. My mother must have observed us together from an upstairs window, but I don't believe she suspected the truth then. She would content herself with long tirades about 'that filthy brat', all of which I ignored, smilingly keeping my silence, for I did not care what she called Alice; the child was not real to me, only the sensations and myths she was able, like a magician, to conjure up.

Alice grew older. She had long passed her eighth birthday, and I was aware that her power over me was waning. Besides she was at times insulting, and had begun now to demand more money: 'Otherwise I'll tell me Mum and Dad.' She stood in the garden, her hand stretched out, grinning perkily up at me. Perhaps it was the heat that summer, perhaps a growing desolation and panic inside of me, knowing that I would have to find some other small companion and not knowing where I would discover anyone so compliant and near at hand as Alice; but one afternoon while we were playing, I unbuttoned my trousers and asked Alice to hold it.

'Cor,' she said, 'I seen bigger than that.'

I quickly buttoned up my trousers again; I was bitterly ashamed. I could not look or talk to Alice again, but worse happened, for my mother had seen something of this episode; not all, certainly, but the truth had entered her mind and she began to watch me closely. She put up a fence between the two gardens, and forbade the Trotter children to cross it, and she then began her campaign to get me married. She pointed out that I was now over thirty and must settle down; when I ignored these mild clichés, her viciousness came to the fore.

'To think,' she spat, 'that a son of mine has the guts of a louse, to think that Francy and I gave birth to a damned snivelling weakling. You and Wilkes,' she'd scream, 'as like as two peas from the same pod. Spinsters both of you, you feeble whimpering neutered things. Ah, what I could tell you of passion.'

I reflected that she had no need to tell me anything, for living with her for thirty years I had observed most of it. She had bitter images that Thomas, whom she had not borne, might be feeling the passion, and laying the whores that I ignored; the fear provoked more assaults upon my sensibility.

'Have you no sex in yuh, does nothing burn, nothing stir? You totter and stutter like an old man. Oh son,' she'd say in a sudden rush of self-pity and feeling, 'I'd known them all at your age, I lost my virginity at thirteen and I was proud of it, yes, proud to begin to explore all the rage and beauty of the world.' Then drawing nearer to me she'd whisper: 'Men, what men I've had, son, what strong beauties, fine wild men who'd make love ten and twelve times of a night. What nights of love and laughter I remember.' Did she ever know how deeply she disgusted me? When I thought of what I had experienced with Alice it seemed the ultimate purity, it seemed to possess a grace and lyrical innocence all the more poignant against her barbaric crudities.

'Saffron May, the belle of the ball;' then she'd attempt to sing, her voice husky with cigarette smoke and gin. 'Sweet Saffron May, how she stole all the hearts away, her fair slim body a sweet bouquet, sweet, dear sweet, Saffron May. . . .' Then she'd weep a little, blow her nose, and look at me with deep discontent. 'You're not goin' to make it in the sack, huh? Y're goin' to be the ruin and despair of me? What ails you, son? You don't have to get married if you don't want to; you got an understanding Ma, why not bring some young lady back home? You've got a nice home. Aren't yuh proud of it? There'd be plenty of gals, I know, who sure would like to live in this house. Besides, we could do with an extra pair of hands about the place.' She looked at me with urgent appeal. 'Lots of men have mistresses, yeah, lots of men; they don't marry, but they still play around.' Then raising her voice: 'You don't seem to even wanna do that.'

For months these tirades continued; she'd try every tactic she could; when one failed she'd employ another, even to the extent of flattery. 'Cuz y're a fine-lookin' fella, maybe yuh don't realize that;' she'd eye my thin concave chest. 'Cuz you're not everyone's cup of tea, but some gals like . . .' she paused, 'thin men, and you've always been quiet, restrained, a true gentleman. . . . That's it, some gals like nice-mannered guys that treat 'em like ladies.'

'I'm happy as I am,' I lied.

'Well, I'm not,' she snapped. 'I give you the freedom of the house, you can fill it with whores for all I care, and what happens? – piss bleedin' nothin'. . . . My God, son, I'd like to wrench the sex from out of you with my bare hands, claw it, damn yer soul, from yer guts and show you the fire in your belly. . . .' She ranted on. 'Yuh scrawny wreck. What woman worth her sex would touch you?'

I didn't know how I could continue enduring such malicious and diabolical tirades; and then it passed through my mind that if I did marry some dull but respectable woman who would have no sexual pretension, not only would it silence my mother, but also be a perfect façade to hide behind for my own secret fulfilments. Once this thought had occurred to me, I saw that the very woman had been there by my side for some years, and I began to look at Miss Clarke in a new light. Not only was she the head secretary of our main Brighton branch and looked after our accounts, but seemed in every way entirely suitable; she could have been aged anything from twenty-five to forty, was correct in her demeanour, wore dull and unattractive clothes, worked hard and was thoroughly reliable; but my difficulty was how possibly to begin even a remote friendship with her, much less propose marriage. But women must have some instinct denied to men, or perhaps she was conscious that I had been staring at her in a new way, for sometimes now she insisted on working late, and we would be left alone. I was in a frenzy of nerves at these times, but she would attempt to converse, drawing me into discussions.

Did I like the countryside? she asked brightly. I had no feelings either way about the countryside, but I thought it best to say I had a great fondness for it. 'Oh splendid,' she said, 'my sister has just bought a cottage near Lewes. I was wondering, maybe one Sunday, well . . . Would you care to drive out there and have lunch with us?' I gladly accepted, and it was arranged that I would pick up Janet at her flat at Dorset Gardens at eleven the following Sunday, to give us time to stop and walk over the Downs. This, I discovered, was more for the sake of her large black labrador than for our pleasure; a dog that acted like a charging rhinoceros for most of the time. 'Playful,' Janet called it.

We drove towards Newhaven, taking the longer route, and stopped the car above Alfriston. I was already thoroughly discouraged; her presence made me feel deeply uneasy; the whole idea of marriage seemed absurd. Surely my mother would finally exhaust herself, and I would be left to lead my life as I pleased. I dreaded getting to the cottage and having to endure the familiarities of a family I did not know or care for.

My feelings changed when I saw Janet's niece, Josie. She was aged five, and full of charm, intensely shy at first, but as I spoke to her gently, she slowly gave me her confidence.

Did I like children? her father asked, beaming down at the child. 'Oh yes, very much.' I saw Janet look at me oddly, as if she was seeing an entirely new person; but that I think is what happened: once in the presence of a child I became transformed, quite gay and comical. Certainly the day seemed a great success. For me, Josie shed magic over the house and landscape, in such a way that I even saw Janet in a different light. Her correct exterior had vanished, and I saw that underneath there existed an infinitely kind and sensitive nature; one I felt would show a patient understanding of my own inadequacies. For the first time in my life it crossed my mind that not all women could be like my mother.

It became an habitual arrangement, our Sunday outing, that summer, and without any words being spoken it seemed to be

tacitly understood by Josie's parents, Jack and Nora (he made furniture and had his own business), that we were engaged. I longed
for those hours, so that I could bask in tiny Josie's presence; there
was no opportunity ever to be alone with the child, and in one
sense I was thankful for this. I knew that, unlike Alice, she would
not allow me to play with her without feeling a form of outrage
which would be immediately communicated to her parents and
thus cause a scandal which my life would never recover from. I told
myself that it was enough just to watch her play and chatter, and
in an odd way it was; I took a delight in her that was quite rarefied.
She was a lovely child with an air of purity about her, so that when
we left I always felt refreshed.

All I had told my mother was that I now visited friends in the
country. I enjoyed her unslaked curiosity, which she could hardly
control. She had recently discovered the cinema, and went to films
three or four times a week, sometimes seeing favourites (always
dramas of strong sentiment) a dozen times or more. *Stella Dallas*
I remember was one. For these trips she insisted upon hiring a
car, and late one afternoon she made a surprise visit to the office.
I saw her arrive, walk slowly through the downstairs rooms and
stare at each female secretary with long intensity, announcing as
she paused who she was. She wore an ocelot coat and a large green
hat I had last seen as a child, plumed with a spray of glossy black
feathers. The impact of her arrival had the desired effect, for she
was finally ushered into my presence by Janet with the kind of awe
given only to Royalty. She plumped her huge crocodile handbag
upon my desk. 'Well, son,' she said, 'which one is it? Come on,
give, boy, which one of those gals will I be saddled with?'

Janet had hardly closed the door, and I was in a state of astonished terror, fearing that if she heard my mother's crude words, she
would refuse to marry me; for by now I had quietened the fears in
myself as to its feasibility. 'Whatever makes you think . . . ?' I tried
to say, but she cut in.

'Lord take your sinful heart, a mother knows when her boy
has turned from her and given himself to another. Son, I've been
patient, but your father's spirit is restless, and truly, I come now at
his request.' She nodded downstairs. 'Who is she?'

What rumours she had heard, or how she had heard them, I

never discovered, or whether she had decided my Sunday absences could only stem from a source at this office. 'It's all, all very uncertain,' I muttered.

'That's a damn lie. Yer father's spirit spoke, and he declared that you'd be married before the fall.' She picked up her handbag and dropped it again upon the desk. 'Glory be, you're a snake in the grass, but you know my nature, son, and I'm just goin' to go down there and ask each one of 'em myself, if you don't introduce me now.' And she sat down, smiling at me and waiting.

I closed my eyes in despair. 'Mother, please, I beg of you, the woman in question would be entirely unprep . . . p . . . p . . . pared.'

She settled herself more firmly in the chair. 'Woman, eh? So, it's not one of those little minxes with an eye on our money. Huh, well, that's something to be thankful for.' Then she paused. 'My Gahd, it's Wilkes junior. Well, son, I'll say somethin' for yuh, yuh certainly play safe. What's her name? Call her in.'

'Miss Clarke is a very nice . . .'

'Call her in.'

I picked up the telephone and asked Janet if she would come into the office; a moment later she walked in, nervously carrying a pad and pencil as if to take dictation, though that was not one of her duties. My mother looked her up and down, her lips pursed in distaste, then she murmured one word: 'Jesus.'

Janet looked at me enquiringly, saying: 'Can I be of any assistance, Mr. Willoughby?'

I swallowed. 'My mother wanted to meet you.'

Janet forced an icy smile. 'Well, now she has.' She turned to go.

'Stop,' my mother roared. 'If you two are gonna make it, I want it done in style.' She leant towards my desk, clutched her handbag, drew it towards her and opened it. She took out a small package. 'Give it to her, son.'

I opened the box; inside was a large emerald and diamond ring.

'Come on now, that's a mighty perty ring, and a family heirloom, though from what side for the life of me I can't recall.'

I handed the box to Janet and began to say: 'My mother wishes . . .'

'Sweet Jesus. Slip it on her finger, son.' She rose. 'And look here,

I don't want any waitin' about. Let's have the ceremony done quick. That's the way I like it, see?'

Janet seemed stunned – as well she might be – and I slipped the ring on to her finger. 'No, no, not that one,' she murmured and placed it on to her other hand.

My mother paused in front of her. 'You sure are a fortunate woman. I just hope you realize the quality of the family you're goin' to join.' Then she clutched the coat about her, nodded to us both and left.

We said nothing. Janet looked at me despairingly, waiting for some word of reassurance. I retreated back to behind my desk. Janet looked at the ring and then at me. 'You did want . . . you did mean . . . ?' I weakly nodded.

There were no words of love, no gestures even between us. I made a clumsy attempt to arrange the formalities of marriage, but then discovered that Janet had a strength of mind I hadn't before suspected. She refused to be married in a church, as she was an atheist, and as to that 'style' my mother had referred to, Janet would have none of it, so my mother refused to attend the registry office or the modest celebration afterwards, which was a great relief to us all. My mother expected us to live at Abbot's Lodge; Janet, who had spent one evening there, said it was out of the question. I was in total and embittered confusion. I pretended to have a sudden allergy to her wretched dog, and maintained that her flat at Dorset Gardens was far too small for us. But I had forgotten that Janet, who had looked after the office accounts for many years, was far more aware of the extent of the prosperity of the firm than I was, and had no misgivings whatsoever in renting a furnished house while we looked for one to buy. She chose a house in the Drive, and after our honeymoon – five days spent in Amsterdam – we returned there. We were complete strangers to each other, and it was terrifying to live in such close proximity with a person I felt only distaste and nausea for.

In Amsterdam I had excused my physical isolation from her by saying that I was suffering from a chill which the perpetual dampness of the air had brought upon me. She tried to show affection; she held my face in her hands and stared closely at me, but I was so taut that she drew back. Thank God she was as ignorant of all physical love as I was, so in those days seemed moderately content to accept my irritability and exhaustion. For I did feel an intense weariness, a feeling of being finally trapped in a form of hell that I had never chosen. My only comfort was the thought of Josie, and I allowed myself to have fantasies that I wove about her. Yet oddly, these were never sexual; I never once thought of her in that way; she was simply an entrancing companion who loved me dearly.

One morning we went out to stroll through the canals; we passed a group of children fishing with bamboos and string, and I dawdled a little behind, for at the edge of the group there was a girl; something – did I imagine it, or was there in the passing look she gave me an instinct of comprehension about my nature? My wife was a compulsive window-shopper, and was hurrying on to the main street. I followed her unwillingly, that tight net of imprisonment heavy upon me. We hesitated in front of windows already festooned with Christmas decorations, then I saw down a narrow alley the entrance to a small baroque church. Her atheist obstinacy was such that she maintained no interest in places of worship. I made my excuses and said that I would meet her later at the hotel. I went down the alley, and saw to my delight that it widened out into a small triangular lawn, surrounded by thin, high, gabled houses, and that there were at least two other exits, one of which might bring me back to the canal where the children had been fishing. I quickened my pace, passed the porch of the church, not caring whether my wife saw that I now ignored it, and turned into another arched alley. I began to run down it, pushing roughly past the phlegmatic Dutch housewives. The alley turned and curved; my leather shoes clattered over the cobbles, and then I saw the grey sheen of a canal in front of me. I was out of breath. I looked up and down it; there was no sign of the children that had been fishing, no sign of the little girl. Indeed, I had no idea whether it was the same canal or another; they all looked so sombrely alike. I hurried along, hoping at every corner I might see them. I passed a sweet shop, paused, then returned and bought some bars of chocolate cream. I hurried on, not caring now in what direction I was going, hopelessly lost, not caring that I would be late back at the hotel, and that I would miss lunch. I had forgotten my nerv-

ous exhaustion, my feeling of being trapped; I felt buoyed up by
hope; surely somewhere in this city I might find the release I so
desperately sought? There were children, certainly; I passed them,
but children clinging on to adults, children in groups, laughing
and shouting among themselves, children that did not notice the
vulnerability of my pleading stare. Oh God, where was she?

It must have been much later that day, well into the afternoon,
for the light was beginning to fail and the city merged into muted
reddish browns as soft as velvet, with an occasional golden glow
from a window, reminding one of the dramatic light in a Rem-
brandt painting, when I saw what I so desperately needed. There
she was, coming out of a bakery, carrying two long loaves in her
brown arms; she was smiling and humming to herself, her thick
black hair tied behind with a yellow ribbon, her skin as dark as
a gypsy. I followed her down the narrow street; then she gave a
little skip, adjusted the loaves in her arms and dropped some of
the change that she had been clutching. The coins ran into the
gutter. I hurried forward, my heart pounding with excitement,
bent down and began to pick up the scattered coins. I pressed
them into her hand, touching her warm fingers for the first time.
I smiled down at her and quickly tried to get the chocolate from
my pocket. She said 'Dank u mijnheer' and hurried on. I followed,
holding the chocolate out to her; she shook her head and took no
further notice of me. If only I had been able to speak her language
I could have held her interest, entertained her, reassured her that I
meant no harm; and what happened afterwards I put down to this
gulf of communication. I looked behind me and saw that the few
people in the street were not near; no one was in front of us, and
I was terrified that she would at any minute disappear into one of
the houses. I picked her up; she cried out, but I smothered the cry
quickly by pressing her face against my coat. One of the loaves fell
at my feet as I turned and ran in a panic down a narrow alley. She
was struggling and kicking, and I saw that the alley led back to a
main street which was bright with lights. I searched the entrances
to the houses either side of us, then saw one with its front door
open and ran up the steps, and found myself in a dimly-lit hall
with a floor of cracked marble; there were doors to either side of
us and a staircase immediately ahead. I took her beneath the stone

stairs; her face was streaming wet with tears and she struggled as fiercely as ever. With one hand I covered her mouth as she bit into my palm, then I fumbled beneath her dress, tearing away at her clothing. I heard myself murmuring absurd words: 'My sweet little treasure, ah, my own darling, my sweet. . . .' and found myself sobbing with relief and fear. Her struggling had suddenly stopped; she lay inert as I felt her nakedness, caressed it again and again, longing for that moment to extend itself throughout my whole life, its cloying heat a subtle mist that obscured in triumph and splendour all the bitter insignificance of the rest of my life. I lost all sense of time and place; the orgasm I knew then made me cry out with the ecstasy of its pain. Then we lay there close together, neither moving; and gradually I became conscious of the sounds within the house: a wireless playing a Beethoven symphony, the sounds of traffic in the city outside. Suddenly I became acutely terrified that the girl was dead, that in suppressing her shrieks I had suffocated her. I took away my hand; her face was very near to mine, then she opened her eyes and stared at me. The eyes were black and huge like enormous vaults, void of sense; their dark emptiness terrified me. I shoved her back against the wall and ran from the house down the steps, kicking aside the other loaf that had fallen there. I ran towards the brightly lit street, but could not endure the light. I ran across it between two trams and into another alleyway, but could not endure that darkness.

I stood by a canal and stared down into the reflections. Barges passed slowly by. I thought I must drown myself. I can have no future. I'm worthless. I walked along the canal searching for a place where there were no people, licking the palm of my hand where the teethmarks had drawn blood; then I saw the hotel. It was half-past six. I leant against a tree and cried.

I told my wife that I had lost myself in the labyrinth of canals and streets, but my clothes were in such disarray and my manner so desolate and wild, that she was acutely suspicious. She pestered me with questions. I said over and over again: 'I don't know. I can't tell;' so that in the end she contented herself with the thought that I had had a lapse of memory and must be ill in some way we hadn't suspected. We cut short our visit and returned to England.

Oh, those terrors in that house in the Drive. I insisted upon us having separate rooms, but she took to coming into my bedroom at night, and would sit upon my bed making all sorts of plans about the house we would buy and how we would furnish it. Then one evening, she looked at me and said: 'Woody dear, you're so fond of children.' She paused uneasily, then suddenly grasped my hand, stroking my fingers. 'Wouldn't you like some of your own?'

I shook my head at once. I heard myself say: 'No, please, no.' She looked at me strangely, and without another word left the room. But oh, women . . . they have this tiresome habit of scratching at a wound, not content with a drop of blood, but continuing to claw until everything runs with . . . is covered with the fury, the endless continuing pain which it seems to me they revel in.

'But it's all so unnatural,' she said sharply. 'Our life, Woody, together; we live a mockery of marriage. What the hell do you want from me?'

'Nothing, please, nothing. . . .'

'It's her fault, isn't it?'

'Whose?'

'Your mother's. Don't deny it, you're terrified of her. Woody, tell me this, my dear, would it be different if we lived with her? Would you then be able to love me?'

'No, no different.' I shook my head in bewilderment. 'Why aren't you content? I don't understand, surely . . . we have this house, you're Mrs. Willoughby now, that's something. Oh yes it is. . . .' I saw her eyes fill with tears.

'Those Sundays . . . at Nora's . . . you seemed so different . . . we all had such happy times together, and . . . I thought I'd found the real you. Christ, I'm made of flesh and blood you know . . . I love you.' And she stumbled towards me, her arms stretched out trying clumsily to embrace me. I moved away and her arms dropped hopelessly to her side. 'You loathe being touched,' she shouted. 'What the hell is it? Won't you tell me?'

I ran from the house, got into the car and drove along the sea front. It was pouring with rain. At Southwick I turned inland, driving through Victorian slum streets. I parked the car outside a school built of red and yellow brick; lights shone from a large Gothic window. A teacher paused there for a moment, staring out at the rain. I got out of the car and walked quickly past the window, and caught a glimpse of rows of heads bent over school desks. I returned to the car and drove on, then stopped at a sweet shop. I drove back to the school, the bulging bag of sweets lying upon the car seat beside me. I passed a policeman on point duty, and the sight of his uniform and cape put me into a panic. No, no, not in this town. I can't, please God no . . . further away, where no one knows me.

Janet had left the office after we were married and now spent her time searching for a house for us to buy. I had a complete lack of interest in it all; it seemed of no consequence where we lived; it was *who* I had to live with that was the only torment. Then she took an obsessive liking to a large white house at the top of Dyke Road. I was dragged to see it and was appalled by its grandeur and vulgarity; built in mock Spanish style, it had an inner courtyard, and a reckless amount of whorled wrought iron. I refused even to contemplate it. She sulked for two days, then finally she said: 'Buy that house and then I don't care how we live.'

'What d'you mean?'

'I mean we'll live separate lives if that's what you want. But I'm damn well going to get something out of this marriage.'

I tried to think, to clear my mind. 'The house is far too expensive.'

She shrugged. 'My God, you've got the money; that's the least of our worries.'

'Wait,' I said. 'Just wait, until after Christmas. It will go down in price. Maybe, then.'

She nodded grimly, then the following day she announced: 'As Nora and Jack are having extensions built on to the cottage I've asked them to spend Christmas with us.' Janet paused. 'Of course if you wish to go to your mother's, I shall understand perfectly.'

My reaction obviously astonished her. 'Splendid, I'll buy a tree and we'll decorate the house.'

'I'm sure your mother won't want to join us,' she said with a frozen smile.

'My mother celebrates whenever she wishes to, and prefers to do it alone.'

She seemed to be mollified by all my excited preparations for this festival. I bought a huge tree and insisted upon decorating it myself, tying several presents upon it for Josie. I lived for Christmas Eve and the time of their arrival, and then when they arrived late, I could not endure the fact that the child was put almost immediately to bed, and the four of us had to spend the long evening without her company. I made the excuse of a severe headache and went to bed early. On my way upstairs, I paused at Josie's room, opened the door quietly, and went in. She slept with her thumb in her mouth and sighed quietly to herself. The whole scene delighted me; the night-light flickered beside the bed sending soft amber shadows over her face and pale gold hair. I was so lost in this enchantment that I did not hear the door open, and Nora's voice in a low cross whisper aroused me: 'What on earth are you doing here?' She tiptoed across to the bed and stared closely down at the sleeping child.

'I thought I heard a cry,' I murmured.

Nora joined me on the landing. 'She's fast asleep.' I suddenly noticed that she was pregnant again; the dress was tight over her stomach and she walked stiffly. Her intensified femininity momentarily disgusted me.

I awoke early the next day and in my dressing-gown crept downstairs and lit huge fires in all the rooms; then I adjusted the decorations on the tree and picked up my presents for Josie and softly went upstairs. The rest of them were still asleep, but Josie was wide awake, sitting up in bed, playing with the contents of her stocking, laughing excitedly. She saw me, stretched out her arms and kissed me on both cheeks; then she unwrapped the huge Mickey Mouse clock I'd given her, and the largest doll I could find. She hugged that, clambered out of bed and began to dance with it. We were both so happy. 'What shall I call her?' she asked.

'You choose.'

'No, Uncle Woody, you must choose,' she said very seriously, a tiny frown of concentration on her brow. I thought for a moment, but was afraid of suggesting any name in case she disapproved. 'D'you think she's ticklish?'

'But of course, all dolls are ticklish.'

She pinched the doll, and as she did so, I crept up behind her and gently tickled her ribs. She went into paroxysms of helpless wriggling and laughter, and tried to tickle me back. We were rolling around the floor, still quite helplessly laughing, when her parents entered the room and discovered us. Their attitude was astonishing; they were immediately angry. Poor Josie burst into tears and I was made to feel guilty. I left the room, trying to appear dignified, but they must have noticed the shame and embarrassment I felt, because they stared at me with distaste and outrage.

The rest of the day was terrible, full of tension and whisperings. What did they know of the purity and innocence I felt for little Josie? What did they think we were doing? Surely they hadn't suspected my true nature? They left immediately after our Christmas dinner, and Janet, after seeing them off, came back into the drawing-room. She stared at me with such loathing.

'I want you to see a doctor,' she said.

Emma

Uncle Woody met me at Brighton Station. We did not go straight back to where I was to live, instead we went into the station buffet and we each had a cup of tea. He scrutinized the teaspoon carefully, adding just half a spoon of sugar, but he stirred his cup thoroughly as if mixing thick paste, and as he did so he watched me intently. When I glanced at him, he would give me a quick, nervous smile; then when we had drunk our tea he patted me on the hand and we left. Outside the station he halted suddenly, grasping my hand tightly.

'Your great-aunt . . .' he began to say.

'But she isn't,' I said at once. 'She's my grandmother.'

'Don't interrupt,' he said petulantly, 'that's just it. There's things you can't understand. She'll be called great-aunt or Mrs. Willoughby.'

'Is it because she's American?' This was all I knew about my father's mother, and it had been told to me as if it were the reason for her strangeness and her harsh behaviour to my father. For it had not been long before that I had questioned my mother as to the absence of any grandparents. My mother had told me of her existence, but had said that she was very ill and had implied that she lived in the United States. I had never bothered to enquire further.

My uncle shook his hand free and replied harshly: 'It would be best if you understood now that it's because of me you're here. Mrs. Willoughby was quite set against you coming at all.' I thought it most odd that he referred to his mother by such a title, and thought again it must be an American fashion. 'And she would only allow it if you're quiet and obedient and fulfil all the requirements she has asked for.' He did not list them then, but suddenly his mood changed, for he knelt down and pinched my arm, then ruffled my hair as if I were his pet dog.

'How about a bag of sweets?' he chanted as he put his hand into his raincoat and brought out some coupons, waving them in front of me. I followed him into the sweet-shop; I waited for him to ask me what I would like but he ordered straight away: 'A quarter pound of humbugs, please. The largest you have.' Then he turned to me and proffered the bag. I took one, though I was not fond of them, and heard him say: 'All little girls love humbugs, don't they?' I sucked it as I stared up at him. 'There, I can see you do.' He ushered me out of the shop and added: 'You're a little humbug yourself, aren't you?'

It became his term of endearment for me, seldom used, for he was a solitary, moody, irritable man.

We caught a fifty-two bus and sat in the front upon the upper deck. I noticed my uncle's hands were deeply stained with nicotine. He was silent, smoking his cigarette, slowly drawing the smoke in and pausing luxuriously. His nose was large and thin, and seemed to travel with too much speed down his face. Perched at the top were thick-lensed spectacles which looked more like goggles. The bus climbed a steep hill, and I looked across the great curved arcs of the station roof traversed by minute ladders – did men really cling to those, I wondered – and saw in the valley a tall church spire, and immediately above it a vast red brick building like a warehouse, but with stained windows. Grey puffy clouds clung to the hills beyond, and then a thin stream of sunlight lit a cemetery. How far? I wondered. What would Monk's Lane be like? It sounded dark and mouldy. What was this list he mentioned? Since I had known that I would be living here, I had protected myself against fear; the unknown and immediate future was blackly threatening, but I felt prepared to suffer any form of ugly unpleasantness as a penance for destroying my mother. The bus passed through a group of shops, passed a huge school shaped like a horseshoe. A boy in a green blazer crossed the playground. The bus went on climbing a long straight hill; I could now see the sea placidly blue on the left. Upon either side there were tall trees that brushed the windows of the bus. I had not imagined it all to be so freshly pleasant, and I felt a momentary elation. Then upon my right I saw a low carved stone building with painted wooden letters which read, 'Bird Museum'. It was in a state of crumbling disrepair, was so low and squat that it disturbed me; the thought of hundreds of birds, once so free, now imprisoned in glass cases, seemed a symbol of what I might have to endure.

It was near this museum that we got off the bus. My uncle led the way down a small side-turning away from the crest of the hill, and then we turned again, into Monk's Lane, a narrow cul-de-sac; and I saw for the first time the house that I was to live in for ten years. A large, spreading cedar tree obscured most of the façade. It had been built in the early years of the century and had two large bay windows either side of the porch. The front garden was wide, but short; most of it containing a curved gravel drive tufted with weeds, ending with wagon-wheel gates bearing the house's name, 'Abbot's Lodge'. I could dimly see that the house was extended either side, but most of these parts were hidden by tall beech and fir trees. A high uncut laurel hedge bordered the garden on all sides. To the right, a high brick wall, flanked by indiscriminately shaped buildings, seemed to be a building merchant's and timber yard. To the left all I could see were other tall and darkly green trees. On the opposite side of the road was a small row of workmen's cottages, their tiny windows heavily obscured with lace curtaining.

Uncle Woody opened the front door. Yes, I thought, his movements did have something of a puppet's jerkiness about them; why did people so often echo their names. The door was panelled with stained glass, of an entwining leaf-and-lily pattern. I meekly followed him into the hall. He nodded to a huge coat-stand; there was an oval mirror at its centre, and as I took my coat off, I stared quickly at myself. My face came to a point – it had always made me anxious; I feared as I grew up this peculiarity would become sharper, and I resented not being a man and being able to grow a beard and so disguise it – now to my dismay, the point of my chin seemed sharper, more rigid and indestructible than ever, as if the tension of my arrival had deformed it more deliberately.

He opened the door of what I supposed must be the drawing-room. 'It's Emma, isn't it?' he enquired. I nodded. 'Wait here.'

I heard him go up the stairs, and somewhere above me, softly, a door opened and closed. It puzzled me that he had to ask my name, for I knew that some months had passed by in a long correspondence between him and the friends of my mother with whom I'd been staying. Perhaps they had always referred to me as 'the child'? I looked about the room; everything was in dark shades of brown and green. I sat down in a leather armchair and waited.

I wondered why my uncle should look and seem so much older than my father; I could see no resemblance in speech or gesture between them at all. I remembered that my father had fine sandy hair, while my uncle was nearly bald.

I did not see my grandmother that day or the next. I heard Wilkes moving softly about the house, and caught my first glimpse of her – a tall thin woman, carrying a glass of water with a slice of lemon bobbing in it – as she went quickly into an upstairs room. I seemed very much to be the charge of my uncle, though he took only a spasmodic interest in what I did.

On that first evening he showed me to my room. He strode up and down it, stroking his chin, then went to the door and abruptly turned to face me. 'Ah,' he said. I was sitting on the bed waiting for him to go. 'You're not . . . now you're not to come downstairs tomorrow morning until I call you.'

I said nothing, but nodded.

He went on: 'You see, child, it's Mrs. Willoughby, she's been so ill.' He sighed as if deeply exhausted himself by referring to it. 'For so long now . . . and people, they get odd. Ah, yes indeed, very odd. . . .'

Perhaps she's mad, I thought.

'And there's certain rules and regulations . . . ah yes, very important those. We all have to live to rules, you see.' And he wagged his finger, but not to me, just to the room itself. Then he shut the door.

My room was upon the third floor, small and with a sloping ceiling beneath the roof; it was at the back of the house and looked across the town towards the east, where on a clear day I could see the race-course. There was a chest of drawers, a cane chair, the bed, and a small table with a china bowl, jug and soap dish.

He did not call me in the morning, but came up to the room. It was past ten, and I had long ago dressed myself and had spent the time staring out of the window. I saw that beneath me there was a domed conservatory and a large overgrown garden. I could hear the trains and see the smoke of the steam-engines spume out, slowly dispersing upwards into the sky.

He nodded to me and I followed him down the three curved flights of stairs to the large kitchen at the back of the house. On the table there was a bowl of porridge and a glass of milk. The porridge was lukewarm, but I was hungry. I ate it quickly as he spoke to me, and I was so pleased to be eating that at first I hardly attended to what he was saying; then I realized that these were the rules and regulations.

'You will not wear shoes in the house, you will keep to the rooms I have already prescribed. . . .'

'Pardon?'

'Your bedroom, kitchen, scullery and garden,' he said irritably. 'You will help Wilkes with the washing and drying-up of all dishes, and you will polish and dust, twice a week, the hall, both landings and the stairs. You will not sing, talk to yourself, or read aloud.'

'May I not bath?'

'Of course, but only once a week, on . . .' He stared down at a piece of paper and squinted at it, then raised his head and said triumphantly: '. . . when my mother says so. All daily washing may be done in the privacy of your bedroom. You will go to Downs School in Dyke Road, about ten minutes' walk from here, and will not dawdle or run on the way there and back.' Then he smiled breezily. 'There, that's not too bad, is it? Of course, I warn you, there's bound to be other restrictions now and again. But we'll have to see how we all get on, won't we?'

There seemed little in the way of an answer I could ever give to my uncle other than a meek nod. None of this appalled me: it seemed that I would have my privacy for long periods, and that was comforting. Besides, all rules were a delight to break, and I secretly promised myself that I would explore every room in the house.

It was almost noon on the third day when my uncle said that he would take me to see my great-aunt. We went from the kitchen to the hall, and there he paused and whispered: 'Do exactly what she asks, be polite and respectful, and address her properly.'

This was confusing. I tugged at his sleeve and whispered: 'Do you mean I'm to say Grandmother?'

He glared down furiously at me. 'I told you before. She's your great-aunt. You must understand that. Is it clear now? Is it clear?'

It was very far from clear, but I followed him up the stairs and noticed that before he knocked upon the door he adjusted his tie and collar.

The sensation of being face to face with this woman for the first time was so great that I was not aware of the room she was in or the objects which surrounded her. Immediately we entered the room I was immersed in the strong stench of lavender and a pungent and sweetly cloying cologne. The huge bed faced the door, but any visitor had to go round a large tapestry screen, so that one faced down the room and did not see at first where the occupant lay. As Uncle Woody prodded me forward, I found myself in a large gloomy room whose colours were all shades of mauve and purple. At the same time I heard the words: 'My, she's a scrawny thing,' in an excessive American drawl. I turned round and saw the huge white-and-lilac bed banked with pillows and drapes, and the vastly fat, painted woman that lay there. 'Pinch yer shoulder blades together, cutie, posture's poor. Well. My, my, son, I can't for the life of me see any resemblance.'

I felt deeply grateful for that, but I was so astonished by her bizarre looks and the harsh crackling sound of her voice and accent, that I could only stare at her in bewilderment.

'Come a little closer. Now, would yuh be fond of peppermint creams?' Her throat gave a spurt of what might be laughter. 'Cuz I'm partial, I've got a sweet tooth. Son, isn't that so?'

I felt my uncle prod me so that I took several steps towards the bed, and heard him say: 'That's certainly true, Saffron.' Then I stumbled upon a step on which the bed was raised; my hand touched the pale gauze of the bedcover and felt the slippery sheen of the silk lining.

'That'll do, that's far enough.' She raised one white podgy hand, noduled with great clusters of rings. 'My, you're awful skinny, and damn me, if her ears don't stick out like a nigger's arse. Well, I must conclude that your Ma was no beauty. Let's just give thanks to the Lord there was only one pup in that litter.'

'I thought . . .' I began to stutter.

'Well, glory be, does the child have a thought and a tongue? Well, son, how's she been?'

'. . . my mother was very pretty,' I insisted.

A slight frown passed momentarily over those deeply powdered brows, but she ignored my remark and went on talking. I could hardly take in the meaning of what they said to each other. Her hair was bright gold, curled and contorted like an elaborate crown on top of her head; her eyelids were bright blue, ending in heavily mascaraed lashes which almost hid eyes that seemed colourless; her scarlet mouth was one huge cupid's bow above and below the natural lips. I could discern no visible neck, for her white powdered cheeks and chins lay on a huge bosom, the expanse of which was added to and accentuated by a mass of frills, lace and tiny purple and pink ribbons.

'. . . I'm mighty particular about personal hygiene in my home,' she was saying. 'I cannot abide dirt in any form or fashion. So I expect you, son, to inspect the child's nails both night and mornin'.'

'You can rely on me, Saffron,' my uncle murmured with what I felt were oddly measured tones.

They seemed now to have quite forgotten that I was in the room. My uncle had seated himself in an armchair and they were passing between them a box of glacé fruits. My great-aunt (for I decided to call her that in my own mind from now on, as I was far too humiliated to own up to myself that this woman could ever have given birth to my father) licked the sticky sugar off each thumb and finger as she chewed and chatted.

'I'm goin' to have new drapes, son. You know I'm so partial to material with life in it. D'you all want me to lie here in a tomb? Well, the good Lord spoke to me last night. I heard Him distinctly, and He told me: "Saffron, you just go and get yourself some new satin drapes." "Lord," I said, "that's a mighty good idea." And I knew immediately that the Lord's colour was gold.'

My uncle leant forward attentively and echoed: 'Gold.'

'That's what he said. So, son, you just go this afternoon and buy me the heaviest golden satin you can find in this town.'

'They'll want to measure the windows.'

'They can measure the ones downstairs, they're the same size, son. You know I can't have strangers enterin' this room. I won't have those spirits disturbed.' Then she looked sharply at me. 'That's kinda strange, Woody, I must have forgotten to tell yuh, but those spirits have been all agog about the arrival of our little Miss here. My, my,' and she shook her huge head slowly, 'what a tangle of confused whisperin' comin' at me from all sides, son, so that my poor sensitive soul's been sorely bruised by all the psychic agitation.'

I saw that my uncle seemed to be alarmed at this statement, but she smiled warmly at him and patted his hand before he could withdraw it. 'My, there's a pert look about her, son. I guess you and she will get along just swell.' She closed her eyes and laid her head back upon the pillows, sighing with contentment.

My uncle rose from the chair, nodded to me, and we left the room.

I had already seen that in the drawing-room there was a large glass-fronted bookcase filled with volumes. I had, on that first afternoon, tried the door and found it locked. Peering through the glass door I could see the collected works of Walter Scott, Robert Louis Stevenson and Charles Dickens, and other names and titles. I promised myself to dedicate every free moment when I was not observed to finding the key, planning to borrow one book at a time and hide it beneath the pillow of my bed. But the drawing-room had been forbidden to me, and it was very much my uncle's preserve. On weekdays he was the only one who left the house and bought our daily requirements. Wilkes went to chapel on Sundays, for she disapproved of my great-aunt's muddled spiritualism and would not attend the ceremony that I and my uncle were forced to endure. I was so shaken and bewildered by my first meeting with my great-aunt that I could not find the courage that afternoon to creep down the stairs and begin the hunt for the key, so I contented myself with a detailed exploration of the floor that I was on. There appeared to be two more rooms other than my own. The first door I tried was locked; there were no other doors facing the front of the house so the room must have included the whole area and be quite large. I bent down and peered through the keyhole, but it was either obscured by something, or the room was darkly curtained. I was annoyed that I had not been given this room, which was obviously twice the size of my own. I then turned the handle of the third door. I peered in, to see a room of similar size to mine. It was filled with old trunks and suitcases. A stuffed alligator a foot long, its liver-coloured mouth open and stupidly grinning, lay on a piece of mahogany on the window-sill. A garland of white wax lilies-of-the-valley lay over the neck of a stuffed pheasant. A sword was hooked upon a wall next to a large turtleshell with a small brass shield screwed at the bottom of its rim. It read: 'In honour of General Norwood T. Willoughby . . .' but the rest of the words had been gouged out and heavily scratched with a sharp blade. I opened one of the trunks; to my delight I saw it was filled with books. They seemed very worn and discoloured, but when I took them out and leafed through the pages, I became discouraged. They were all ancient school-books – Latin, French, Geometry and Algebra; on all of the fly-leaves was written in copper-coloured ink and in a curled script: 'Francis Norwood Willoughby'; the dates were late in the last century. In another suitcase I found only framed pieces of embroidery, a sepia-coloured photograph of some soldiers upon horses, some medals and war ribbons, and a newspaper given over completely to the *Titanic* disaster, which I sat down and read. I was about to leave, when I saw, pushed into another corner, a suitcase more exotic than the others, as it was covered in crimson plush. I hauled it out. It was small, with crocodile straps which I quickly untied, but its contents were just as disappointing: it was crammed with garishly covered books of young wilting heroines and blank-faced young men with their hair centre-parted, staring at posturing girls with amazed admiration. I turned the books over and discovered a photograph lying at the bottom. I saw a very handsome young man in evening dress and wearing a top hat at a mischievous angle, leaning upon a cane and staring at the camera with audacious but smiling content. The mouth was dark as if reddened by paint, and the hands were slender and as fragile as a woman's. Then I saw the faded inscription, scrawled over one corner. I deciphered with difficulty: 'The maddest love, darling Sadie.' Quickly I searched for more photographs, but failed to find any more. There were still other suitcases to open and explore, but I was afraid to stay too long.

'Wilkes is the poor relation,' my uncle said. We were in the kitchen eating lunch: a slab of spongy cod that had been boiled with carrots, and mashed potatoes that tasted of earth. This was his introduction to Wilkes, who disregarded what he said and barely looked at me. I wondered whether I, too, came into this category? 'You'll learn, child, that some of us are born to lead, and others only to serve. Wilkes here, of course, ought to belong to the latter, but her brain is the size of a pea,' and he stabbed a piece of carrot and popped it into his mouth, then he chuckled. 'Maybe you think she might manage to serve the servants, but she makes a dreadful hash of everything.' If she was so inadequate, I wondered, why did my great-aunt keep her on?

Tentatively I asked: 'What is wrong with my great-aunt?'

My uncle paused, placed a piece of fish in his mouth and swallowed it. 'Heart.'

'Is she very old?'

He took the butter knife and rapped me across the knuckles. I withdrew my hands to my lap. 'Don't ask impertinent questions.'

The rest of the meal was finished in silence; then my uncle rose and left the kitchen, leaving Wilkes and me to clear up the dishes. I stood beside Wilkes in the scullery and dried the plates carefully. Her tiny wrinkled head was bent over the sink; her knuckles were bright red against the pallor of the rest of her skin.

'What kind of relation would you be?'

'No relation,' she murmured in the worried staccato way she talked. 'No relation at all.'

I felt that in this house no one seemed to be what they were called. 'But why does he say that you're . . . ?' I hesitated to use his phrase.

She carefully rinsed beneath the tap the especially thin china that my great-aunt used, then she looked up and stared out at the conservatory where a gnarled vine grew with stunted purple grapes like pellets. 'I was brought up as one of the family.'

'What family?'

'The General. Oh, he was an odd one, though old Mrs. Willoughby was as kind as you'd ever find. The army and the scandal broke 'em both, though they lived so far out in the wild no one around there knew it was the same Willoughby. Mister, they all called him. That hurt him.'

She went on washing the china; there seemed to be so many fascinating strands of knowledge here that I hardly knew which one to follow, and I was terrified that she might lapse into her former dour silence.

I took a deep breath. 'What relation would I be to the General?'

Wilkes shook her head and used the mop vigorously. She seemed to be enclosed in her own memories, for when she spoke again I couldn't at first understand.

'Sold I was,' she said with sudden vehemence, and waved the mop aloft. 'Too many mouths to feed. Fisherfolk they were and dying yearly in the storms. But old Mrs. Willoughby needed help in the house.'

We hadn't been aware that my uncle had come silently back into the kitchen and had been listening. We heard him shout: 'You cretinous old dunce-head. Stop filling the child's mind up with your fuddled rubbish.' Then he took my hand and pulled me away. Wilkes trembled and hunched herself farther over the sink. We stood together in the doorway.

'Sold indeed,' he said sarcastically. 'Your father was a drunk, and your mother left her brood of little brats behind and went off with the gas man. Fine stock you came from.' Then he shoved me back through the kitchen. 'Up to your room, now.' As I left I heard him say: 'Now, I don't want you burbling away to her again. Is that understood, Wilkes? If my mother heard of it. . . .' His words tailed off, but I heard Wilkes sobbing.

I began to climb the stairs, depressed not so much by my uncle's harshness as by the fact that now it seemed I would hear no more stories, however confused, that linked up with some of the objects in the attic room. I wondered whether Wilkes knew who Sadie was.

Suddenly I was face to face with a huge tabby cat. It sat at the head of the stairs calmly licking its paws and staring at me as I stood some steps below. I liked animals, so I stretched out my hand and made 'pussy' noises. It stopped washing itself and stared back at me. There was a wound on the side of its face, still coagulated with blood, and one ear was flattened and misshapen. It made no sign of sensuous pleasure, and I felt more disturbed by its stoic stare than by any other event since I had arrived.

I decided to ignore the cat, and climbing another stair, was preparing to pass it, when it arched its back, its fur sprang up so that suddenly it seemed twice its size, and it hissed. Almost at the same time my great-aunt's hand-bell began ringing, and she began

to call: 'Bessie, Bessie, where is that damn gal?' Then more ringing and the same cry. The cat turned, and with a haughty whisk
of its huge tail, padded softly down the landing, then jumped up
on to a window-sill and sat behind a heavy lace curtain, staring
down at the street below. The ringing continued as Wilkes passed
me, running up the stairs and into my great-aunt's room. 'There's
some damn thing sticking into me, if only you had the pain I have,
you'd . . .' The voice faded as I went into my room.

After that first meeting, the cat never exhibited any more
aggression towards me; it was as if he wanted to show me that we
were natural enemies and must always remain so.

Down School was privately owned by Miss Tempest, and I
suppose was considered to be select, for there were never more
than sixty pupils, and only two other teachers. Miss Tempest was
extremely tall, with a mole on her large chin that sprouted one
long black hair. She looked like Tommy Trinder. But Miss Tempest
was never intentionally comic. She taught Religious Instruction,
History and English. Her voice often trembled with emotion, for
she had a tendency to relate from the past only stories of heroines
who were fated for some gory martyrdom; we became very bored
with Joan of Arc, Mary Queen of Scots and Nurse Cavell. Both
Miss Hacket and Miss Dobson were of an abnormally short stat-
ure, so that at morning assembly, when we all stood for the hymn,
we christened them 'Tommy and His Dwarfs.'

One morning when a school inspector arrived, we were
delighted to discover that he bore a certain resemblance to Will
Hay. The whole class shook with suppressed giggles as he and Miss
Tempest both promenaded pompously through the space between
the desks. When they left, hysterical laughter finally overcame us,
quickly to be crushed by tiny Miss Dobson, who flew in with a
flurry of woolly limbs, begging us in mime to be silent.

I had no close friends at this school, for I was too intensely
embarrassed to take anyone of them back home. But I soon discovered that 'the rules and regulations' were extraordinarily vague. I
was free to come and go from the house and could wander about
Brighton as I pleased. If I was absent from tea, or even any other
meal over the weekend, my uncle accepted that I must have been

at the house of some school friend. I think the reason for his calm in this matter was his intense meanness, for the small amount of food not eaten at any one meal was saved and served again until no scrap was left. But quite by accident I had discovered a source of income, and over the years I helped myself from it.

I first looked for the key to the bookcase in the drawing-room behind the clock on the mantelpiece, then in a large flower vase; I discovered it the third time in an empty cigarette box. It was an enormous joy to choose a book, then shift the other volumes along the shelf so that they obscured the empty space. For many months I had ignored the largest volume of all, in the corner of the bottom shelf; but though it was a Bible, the heavily tooled leather of its binding one afternoon took my interest, and I pulled it out of its place. It contained amongst its pages countless numbers of pound notes. As I was given no pocket money – one of the rules of my great-aunt who kept the accounts – I felt justified in my secret stealing.

'The poor relation took two boiled potatoes. Watch her, child.' We sat at the huge, scrubbed kitchen table, and I watched the whorls of wood – the knots in it were like islands of soil in an expanse of grainy sand – not daring to look at Wilkes, whose mouth slopped over at the edges like a slab of butter in the sun. I stared at the boiled potatoes, furry at the ends, then down at her wrinkled stockings.

'The poor relation was once in love,' Uncle Woody said, 'with a fiddler at the Grand Hotel.'

I knew the story well, for Uncle Woody delighted in retelling it.

'Awfully posh, and well in his prime. He led her a terrible dance, with a wife in Bognor and a waitress at the end of the pier. The poor relation had no idea she'd suffer and cry so that her ginger hair grew thin and the cyst on the right eyelid swelled up.' I had never observed that Wilkes' hair might at one time have been ginger.

The saga grew as he retold it, adding a morbid detail here and there. Wilkes stood making the tea, holding the caddy up to her ear and shaking it – did she think of India? So far away her look; the thin tissue of her life contracted back into space and time. She remained deaf and mute to his words.

'And one case full of tattered shreds of handkerchiefs she'd torn with her teeth in the night, lying on her iron bedstead, flat and thin as a bone, tearing, tearing.'

Bartholomew, the cat, slept and ate in my great-aunt's room, but at night would pad along the gutter, climb the attic windows and peer in. His eyes were orbs of bubbling discontent. His coat, flecked with fiery points, silhouetted against the cold faceless glare of moonlight, provoked restless nightmares, all of them centred around my great-aunt and the ceremonial of noon on Sunday, when I would be ushered into her presence to read a psalm of her choice. I did not understand what the words meant, for she had censored this copy of the Bible, so that some phrases were struck out, while other words had been pencilled in. Her favourite passages from the Psalms, Genesis and the Song of Solomon I got to know by heart. 'Ministers with their armies were horrified and their households divided. Though ye have lain among the gold, yet shall ye have the wings of the dove that is covered in copper and her feathers like dross.'

I felt that the Lord God must have some plan of profound importance in keeping Saffron May Willoughby alive and, I supposed, rich; that there was in fact some secret alliance between them, and that if I failed to elevate my voice into the chant, Bartholomew would claw and chew at my tongue. In my nightmares visited by his feline presence, I could not scream, but remained rigid, like a pressed flower in an iron-clasped Bible.

'But the dove found no rest and she returned with him into the sacred house for the waters were upon the face of the earth: then he put forth his hand and took her and pulled her unto him into the sacred house.'

On some occasions she would interrupt me. 'Oh bless the Ones that see all, amen. Oh come, cosmic souls, oh come,' then she would close her eyes and sigh deeply.

'I sleep, but my heart waketh: it is the voice of my beloved that knocketh, saying, Open to me, my sister, my love, my dove, my defiled.'

I would not have to read aloud for long before I was sent away, but I would still hear her voice and his for a long time afterwards, pitched in curious cries. This was when I could converse with

Wilkes, for she had returned from chapel by the time I came down the stairs. For many months after my uncle's anger she had refused to speak to me, but with persistence I wore her down, for I think she was longing to talk to someone, and especially about the past. No one I ever knew lived such a thin and inadequate existence. When she was not tending the invalid, she stayed in the room next to the bathroom and across the landing from my great-aunt, and only appeared in the kitchen to prepare our meals. On Sundays she would place a joint of meat in the oven before she went out; when she returned I helped her prepare the vegetables. I took my time peeling the potatoes and inspecting each brussels sprout with careful scrutiny, while my mind was elsewhere, asking questions that might ferret out tiny shreds of information. I was exploding with curiosity. 'Did you ever meet my father?' No answer. 'When he was my age, did he live here?' Silence again. 'Why was my great-aunt so horrid to him?' She sighed. 'Why is my uncle so much older?' She shook her head. 'Why won't she be called grandmother?' Silence. 'Do all Americans look like that?'

Her obstinate silence was total, and it was finally broken by an accident. I had begged to be allowed to put the peeled potatoes into the oven tray of hot fat, and when I opened the oven door, instead of placing them in, I dropped them, so that the fat splashed up and scalded my hand. Wilkes was suddenly all concern, taking my hand as I cried out. She placed it under the cold water tap, then patted it dry and rubbed it with lard, all the time mumbling away in her tremulous tones a spate of words that I could hardly follow.

'There, there, just like me. Why I couldn't use my arm for a week, and old Mrs. Willoughby herself waited on me hand and foot, and even took the trap and drove it herself down to the village to buy the things we needed, and special things too, all kinds of sweets and delicacies, and nicely laid out, special, on a tray, so that I felt like a little princess, and my, she shut the General up then, she did.'

I looked down at my hand with its scarlet splodges, and the thin rough fingers shiny with fat that smoothed the pain away. 'Why, Wilkes, whatever happened?'

'Burnt myself, horrible, I did,' and she rolled up the sleeve of her blouse and showed me her forearm. A long weal of puckered skin went from just above her wrist to her elbow. Even now, it seemed like a savage wound.

I felt chastened, and whispered: 'How did it happen?'

'With a red-hot poker.'

'Did you fall?'

She bent her head close to mine. 'Fall, nothing, 'twas the General in a rage again. So many clocks in that house, why everywhere you looked, and he as fierce about the actual second everything was done. They never kept much staff for long, I tell you that. Tick, tock, tick, tock, all over the house, morning, noon and night. . . .'

'But the poker?' I tried to remind her, for I was longing to know the actual drama of the scene, but I learnt afterwards it was of no avail to try to guide her thoughts. I had always to be patient and hope she would return to the original impetus that had set her memory alive.

'. . . woken by a bugle, the whole house – him, with snow-white whiskers and eyes as bright as bluebells. Always wore his uniform for dinner, every night, and that had to be brushed and pressed with the buttons polished first thing of a mornin'. One might have never thought it of him; except when he died the papers talked and the vicar of those parts came to see old Mrs. Willoughby with a copy of *The Times* tucked in his riding-coat; just this side of the Tamar we were. . . .'

'But why was he so angry with you?'

'. . . and I heard somethin' of what they said, for I believe truly then that I was a comfort to her, cos she was more troubled, poor soul, at what the papers said, than him at last leaving this sorrowful world, so I found out then he'd had 'em murdered. . . .'

'Who?'

'. . . thousands of 'em, I believe . . . the blacks, strung up in every corner of that island, cos one of them killed a soldier. But Lord love us, 'twas early in their marriage, and she stuck by 'im, though somethin' died in that poor woman, for she only bore him one son, late in life, but that's another story. . . .' She suddenly stopped, staring at the kitchen dresser with its display of white and orange cups, bowls and platters. She sat next to me, her bare arm lying on the table. Tenderly I touched the wound and felt the still-puckered skin, fascinated by its paleness against the yellow arm

with moles like brown stitches. She unrolled the sleeve and buttoned the blouse at the wrist, then looked up at the kitchen clock.

'Ah, everything had to be done on the minute. I was late bringin'
the coals in. Well, it was a bitter winter and I had to go through
the yard. I can see the snow now. We'd be cut off for weeks and
that's why old Mrs. Willoughby was as brave as they come, taking
the trap and fighting her way through that weather, though I do
believe she told me once she was born in India, the daughter of a
colonel. It took me time searching for enough bits of coal to fill
the scuttle, but I couldn't have been more than ten minutes. Five
he liked it, then again after dinner, eight-thirty. To bed at ten and
up again at six. I'd rolled me sleeves up high, you see, so the cuffs
wouldn't be dirtied. He was on his knees shouting and poking the
fire.' She sighed.

'Was Francis their son?'

She nodded. 'That's right, your own grandfather. He was a dear
man.'

Then we heard my uncle's step in the hall.

On the last day of every month, my uncle went out early in
the morning and disappeared all day. There seemed to be an extra
ceremonial at these times. He would stand in the hall and first
of all inspect the high, carved hallstand; his umbrellas, walking
sticks, hats and several overcoats seemed sombre and managerial
against my thin green school gaberdine and the dented pudding-
basin hat I was forced to wear. He would consider his coat before
wearing it, as if some minor transformation had occurred in the
night: carefully he tested each button to see if it was secure, then
allowing the hem to touch the floor he would adjust the sleeves,
frowning down at the lining. He placed his grey homburg on and
stared in the mirror to see if it was exactly level, then taking either
an umbrella or a stick with one hand, he'd pick up a large briefcase
and leave. I longed to know what was in the case.

One afternoon, believing he was still out of the house, I quietly
entered the drawing-room and had half-crossed it, before I realized that he was seated at a roll-top desk behind me in the corner
engrossed in counting up a list of figures. He had not heard me
come in, for I had disciplined myself to creep around the house

with as much stealth as Bartholomew. But I feared to return, for any movement I made now might draw his attention. I stood very still and tried to imagine what excuse I might have for being here, but my mind was unusually blank. He finished his addition, and taking a ruler, pencilled a line at the bottom of the page, then reaching down to the briefcase he took out a bundle of one-pound notes and began to count them. I had left the door ajar, and now I saw that Bartholomew had followed me into the room. The cat began to claw at the sofa and my uncle looked up. He looked quite astonished, and said nothing for a moment, then his face flushed with anger and he shouted: 'Get out.'

Later that same day, he called me back into the room. I prepared myself for a tirade, but his mood had quite changed. He had a glass of sherry in one hand and was smoking a cigar, and he walked slowly about the room in an expansive, almost jolly mood. He told me to sit down. Then he waved one hand and said: 'One day, all this could be yours.' Did he expect me to be thrilled by this prospect? My great longing was to grow up as quickly as I could and to leave this house and never return.

'You saw the money? That's a lot of money, isn't it? Yes, well, I'll tell you, it is a lot of money, and every month of every year the same amount of money is collected by me and put into a bank. D'you know where it comes from? Of course you don't. Well, I'll tell you.' He sat down upon the sofa, leant back, and drew at his cigar. 'Property. That's where. Property? Houses, land, yes, property.' Then he made another wide gesture of his hand which seemed to encircle the world. 'The Willoughbys own all this around here. Streets and streets of it, and not only here, but in other counties as well. Doesn't that make you proud to belong to a family that's something in the world?'

I thought of the red-hot poker wielded by my great-grandfather and the blacks he'd slaughtered; did it all mean the ownership of rows of dismal little workmen's cottages? Then he leant forward, jabbing the cigar towards me. 'I married once, you know,' he laughed with self-mockery, 'taken in I was, I can tell you. She married me for my money. Never again. Wouldn't live here. Wanted a big new house at the top there, set her mind on it, done in Spanish style it was, too grand by half. It's vulgar to exhibit your wealth, I told her. But I'd married beneath me. Saffron knew it, but she didn't say.' Then he ground the cigar out viciously in the ashtray and said furiously: 'She egged me on, yes, made me marry, insisted upon it. You'd think, wouldn't you, that a mother would consider her son more. But no, she wanted to humiliate me, make me suffer all the indignities that, that . . . shrew . . .' he spat the word, '. . . inflicted on me.' He lapsed into sudden silence and sipped the sherry. 'I'm not strong, you know,' he went on thoughtfully. 'Never have been. The doctor said I'd got a small heart. Can't do the work it should. D'you know what my chest measurement is? Thirty-five and one quarter. Like a boy's.' He grunted, then began to hum a tune, and with his fingers he beat out the time on the arm of the sofa. 'Back there,' he nodded behind him, 'we own all that. Trotter's place at the end of the garden. When I was a boy, the servants lived there.' He paused and looked a little uneasy. 'Used to make puppets, you know, when I was young. Clever with my hands I was. But a man can't. . . . There comes a time. . . . Well . . .' His words trailed away into a long silence. I sat there, not knowing whether I was to leave or stay. I started to look around the room, though I knew each sombre piece of furniture well. When I turned again to look at him, his expression had changed again: he was staring at me with a look of such vulnerable appeal that for the first time since I had met him I felt something akin to affection and wanted to sit near him, though what pain or confusion he was suffering which had produced this look of naked emotion I was too young to understand. But suddenly he shook his head like a swimmer surfacing, rose, and poured himself out another glass of sherry. While his back was turned away from me, I heard him say softly: 'You're not a bad child. Go now. Off with you.'

I sat on the floor of the junk room, surrounded by displaced trunks and suitcases, by now all of them in a new confusion, re-arranged by the ardour of my explorations. I had discovered other faded and torn photographs of the ubiquitous Sadie Stirling in an endless range of costumes and poses: in crinolines and farthingales looking like Catherine the Great or Marie Antoinette, or posed in Edwardian grandeur with a wasp waist, a huge bust and behind, simpering beneath vast hats and holding huge bunches of flowers.

Some of the photographs were labelled with what seemed like titles of plays; others had glowing messages scrawled upon them. I had already asked one of the schoolgirls, who was an ardent film fan, whether she had ever heard of this actress. She looked at me quite blankly, as if I were creating a myth, and the wretched name stuck to me for many months afterwards as an excuse for their teasing. I decided that Francis must have had a consuming obsession for her. It never crossed my mind to ask Wilkes to shed any light on this puzzle, for I could not imagine anyone further removed from the theatre; besides I treasured Sunday mornings and the confidences she gave me, for we had begun to trust each other, though neither of us dared show it to my uncle. It was odd, I reflected, that though Wilkes was so frightened and cowed throughout all the mundane duties of her life, when she spoke to me of the past she seemed to gain a perky strength and brightness, so that her tiny face became quite transformed; and quite unconsciously, I am sure, as she spoke, she would tidy herself up, take her spectacles off, polish them briskly, adjust her collar, re-pin a brooch, smooth her dress and stroke her sparse hair. She even spoke of the fiddler at the Grand Hotel.

'I would never have dreamt of it, you see. But it was Mr. Willoughby who encouraged me. . . .'

'Francis, you mean?'

'Now that was odd, kindness itself he was, like his mother before him. You see, he was a lonely man. You'd think, wouldn't you, that he had everything to live for. All that money and so much in love, but she . . .' Wilkes trembled a little and lowered her voice, 'she gave him a terrible dance. But never a cross word he'd say. Patient like a saint, and kind, as I've said, to all of us, he was. Lost a lot of money through her, he did. . . .' Then with sudden excitement, she said: 'I'll tell you what kind of man he was: came here to look after his old nanny.' And she sat back. 'There. Course I looked after his mother until she went, God bless her soul. Then he said: "Bessie, you come and live with us and not a stroke, no, not a stroke are you going to do."' She smiled; a sudden sweetness lit her features, and I could suddenly see that when she had been a girl she must have been quite pretty. 'And what's more, I didn't. No, and that's when he told me I had to get about a bit.

"Enjoy life", he said.' She paused. 'It was the happiest time of my life, I can tell you, Emma, I only hope you'll have such happy times as I did then.' She smiled again, began to hum very softly a waltz.

'What did you do?'

'Why, every afternoon I'd listen to them play. I'd sit there in the same chair and the same waiter would bring me a pot of tea on a tray and assorted cakes. Oh, another waiter brought those, wheeling them on a trolley. Any amount of cakes you could have.' And she began to hum again. '"Bessie", he said, "get your hair done, buy yourself some clothes." He was a real gentleman, he was, I can tell you.' She stopped and looked suddenly sad.

'My father, did he live here then?' I asked quietly.

Her body twitched suddenly. 'There, that's when I was silly, all dressed up as if I was a lady, smart hat and handbag. Well, as I said, Mr. Willoughby wanted me to look nice, but it all went to my silly old head. I should never have written him a letter.'

'Who? Who did you write to?'

'Oh, if only you could have seen him, Emma. Albert was his name, and he played beautifully. He had black curly hair, a little moustache and the whitest teeth I've ever seen on any man. He answered my note very politely . . . oh yes, he was always the soul of respect, and asked me to meet him at a tea-shop just at the corner of East Street.'

'Did you go?'

She shook her head. 'Oh no, I was in such a state. I told Mr. Willoughby what I'd done and he just laughed. I couldn't go back there, not for a week, and I did miss the music so, but Mr. Willoughby, he told me not to be such an old silly, that there was nothing wrong in friendship, and that's all it was, he said. So, one afternoon he went along with me. There, maybe that gave the wrong impression, because they all knew who he was, and he had a manner about him – you know – oh yes, they were all very attentive – and Albert . . . well, he smiled at me, but I couldn't look at him, I felt so flustered and ashamed.' She took a tiny handkerchief from her cuff and wiped her eyes. 'Gracious me, I could have sunk through the floor when Albert came right up to our table, nodded to Mr. Willoughby and said to me: "I was afraid you must have been ill." He sat down and chatted to us, but for the life of me I can't remember what was said.'

She rose and turned the gas-ring off, pouring the saucepan of greens into a colander. Her stories would always end abruptly, as if her total remembrance of the past suddenly became too strong for her to endure.

The back garden was overgrown and wildly tangled, for there was no one to tend it. The fruit trees were large and barren, still solemnly carrying dead and rotting limbs, their trunks hidden by coarse brambles that might once have carried luscious loganberries or been heavy with the sweet scent of roses. I would hear Mr. Trotter complain with bitter resentment, for there was no wall or fence between this rank confusion and the exact symmetry of his own small back garden where bright flowers grew in exact rows around the small patch of lawn. I would peer through the tangled skein of privet and laurel, watching him crouched and bending, muttering with spinster fussiness as he wielded his trowel. It would flash silver with the sunlight, for he took as much care and trouble over his gardening tools, stacked carefully in a green-painted lean-to shed, as he did over the plants. He was a short man, with thick strong limbs, and I learnt afterwards that he worked as a porter down at the station. I was not fascinated with Mr. Trotter himself, but rather with the elaborate painstaking care of his labour. No one else I knew cared for anything outside themselves, unless I counted my great-aunt and her love for Bartholomew. It was the cat that made me love Mr. Trotter.

Wilkes had burnt the Friday scones. This had driven Uncle Woody into a temper; he threw the teapot at Wilkes, and it smashed above her head. I had run from the kitchen, through the scullery and out into the conservatory. Wilkes had followed me sobbing in fear; and because the conservatory gave no shelter, and since my parents' death I had had a terror of jagged glass, I ran further on, down through the garden; and breaking through the tight labyrinth of knotted shrubs, I began to squeeze my way into a space where I could not be seen. I crouched uncomfortably on the dank soil. I could hear Uncle Woody's voice still raised hysterically. Mr. Trotter came out of his kitchen door, carrying a seed tray of cuttings. He must have heard the noise, but he seemed to take no notice. I watched him carefully, drawing comfort from his leisured serenity. I saw how his large hands with their splayed thick fingers had the precision of a pianist, as delicately he took each cutting and, cradling its earth-clogged roots in the palm of his hand, he gently laid it down, then carefully pressed the earth around it so it stood supported and exactly upright. As I watched, the spotted scarlet blur of a ladybird moved across the framed picture of my gaze, not two inches away. Its fragile legs, I noticed for the first time, were the colour of used tea-leaves. For a moment I forgot about Mr. Trotter and watched the ladybird's progress; then in a salmon-pink haze of industry, its shell parted, and it flew upwards, through the dark leaves, and I followed its flight for a moment, suddenly conscious that the noise from the house had stopped and that some other sinister presence was there.

Near where I crouched a silver birch grew. I was aware that some seconds before I had heard a slight noise. Slowly I turned my head, and felt a sudden horror. Bartholomew was crouched upon a branch, watching me with his sunset eyes of liquid fire, staring down at me with the same intensity I had had when watching the ladybird. I drew back further into the undergrowth, but because now I had discovered him, he seemed bored, and began to move away from me across the tree, and jumped down upon the wall that divided Mr. Trotter's garden from a building yard next door. I believed that Bartholomew could communicate with my great-aunt, and inform her of all he saw, for the way she clung and petted him, so indifferent to his disdainful outrage, seemed to imply always a hungry need in her for his secret knowledge.

I watched him as he padded silently away. There was no sign of Mr. Trotter. I wondered whether I could return unnoticed, creep in and ascend the back stairs which were used only by Wilkes, but to reach my own room meant passing Uncle Woody's. Bartholomew stretched himself and yawned. I saw the livid cavern of his mouth, fringed with needle teeth, and wondered regretfully why in butcher's shops they slaughtered the docile lamb and never cats. A butterfly hovered above a sunflower head, then alighted for a moment, its white wings reflecting the yellow glow of the seed heads. Then it flew down, brushing across multi-coloured dahlias.

Suddenly there were two of them, touching each other, dancing in the warm air of that August evening. Bartholomew had seen them too, and lightly he leapt down onto Mr. Trotter's lawn. The butterflies swung high; the cat appeared to be uninterested, now slumped upon his haunches and cleaning his white belly. Then I saw Mr. Trotter. The top part of his kitchen door, though neatly paned, was separate, as in a stable, and this was wide open. He stood in his kitchen, most of his squat body shrouded in shadow, but I could see his face clearly and it was blotched – like Uncle Woody's often was – with patches of red fury. He stared at Bartholomew, who had stopped his pretence of washing and was slyly watching the butterflies which had flown lower. I saw that slowly Mr. Trotter was raising his right hand, and it was poised with the same precision he had used in gardening; but could not see what he held. I saw the hand move slowly backwards, then with an abrupt forward movement his fingers opened, and an object flew straight and sudden towards Bartholomew. Though the cat's attention was elsewhere, his instinct was quickly sensitive; hearing it in the air, he swivelled about, squawking with fright, and the steel-pointed dart hit the lawn between his front paws. He flew, making for the fence that bordered the other side of the garden, and as his claws clung to the wood, another dart thudded next to him. Mr. Trotter came running out, chuckling with delight. Bartholomew has disappeared. I was delighted, and wondered whether Mr. Trotter and I could be friends.

It was some weeks after this that I was alone, seated in the kitchen, reading a library book by G. A. Henty – I believe it was the one about the Spanish oppression in the Netherlands – I was quite lost in this story; it fulfilled the deep emotional longing for freedom in my own imprisonment. But I was conscious that some tiny detail in the ordered routine of the house was amiss. I looked up at the kitchen clock; it had a painted glass panel beneath it of a gondola upon a Venetian lagoon, except the paint had peeled where the water should be, and the gondola floated above the interior brass mechanisms. The clock stubbornly ticked, but it was past five, and at four-thirty every afternoon Wilkes entered the kitchen and prepared Great-aunt's tea-tray. I realized at the same time that I was thirsty and had heard no sound from upstairs that whole afternoon. This was not unusual immediately after Sunday dinner, for they all dozed for an hour; but often at about three, Uncle Woody and I would play dominoes. I shut the book, took a glass and filled it with cold water. The scullery tap made a clonk and an asthmatic coughing noise when you first turned it, and if you continued to turn it back and forwards so that it never gushed out, it made all kinds of variations: like a heavy marching boot thumping on a pavement, sometimes like corrugated iron rattling in a fierce wind; sometimes, if you persisted, it squeaked with exhaustion, then sighed as if one were being wantonly cruel. I played with it then, comforted by its rusty noise. I knew that if I continued long enough, Uncle Woody would appear, shouting at me to stop, for the noise travelled through the plumbing of the house, and tiny spurts of water would leap up from the upstairs basins.

But I tired of the game, and no one appeared. The clock said a quarter past five. I put the already filled kettle upon a gas-ring and lit it. The flames flared vicious blue. Then somewhere above me I heard the sound. I listened carefully and ran to the kitchen door, my ear placed close to the panelling. It was such a mixed odd sound. I opened the door a little. Yes, it was Uncle Woody, and he appeared to be laughing; but also there was another kind of laughter, high-pitched and quite hysterical; a woman's laughter. The noise of the gas was so harsh that I could not hear clearly enough. I turned it off and opened the kitchen door wide, standing there for a moment, listening and quite bewildered, for there was no doubt now that it was uncontrolled, wild laughter. My curiosity led me up the stairs and into the hall. The sound never abated except for sudden gasps of breath, and my uncle's expressions of 'oh, dear me, dear me'. I ran up the stairs until I could see the whole of the upper landing. My uncle and Wilkes were spreadeagled upon the polished floor, the rugs all awry and crumpled beneath them, both of them holding on to each other and shaking with helpless laughter, their mirth so oddly maniac. Wilkes' grey hair had come undone, and lay like tawdry spider-webs over her thin shoulders, and as her bones shook the hair quivered. I noticed how few teeth she had, and that they were stained. One hand nervously clutched at her blouse, tugging at the worn jabot of lace. I stood there, watching them both, seeing the slack mottled skin of my uncle's throat jolt and agitate as it disappeared into his collarless striped shirt. One hand thumped the floor; the noise was deafening, and my great-aunt had always insisted upon complete quiet. Then they both saw me, but for a moment the sound continued. Then my uncle pulled himself upright and slowly, except for tiny burps of chuckles, the laughter subsided. I watched with amazement as he bent down and extended his hand; he now lifted Wilkes to her feet. She brushed the dust from her skirt and smoothed out the creases.

'Hallo, humbug, want your tea, then?' He smiled down at me with an air of mischief and naughtiness I had never before seen.

I returned to the kitchen and pretended to be engrossed in my book, as both of them followed and made the tea. I cradled my head in both hands and dimly read the same paragraph again and again, taking quick glances at both of them when they seemed not to be aware of me. Wilkes had almost an air of coquetry about her, as she warmed the teapot, dabbing at the untidy strands of hair which she had only clumsily pinned. My uncle began to slice and butter the bread; I had never seen him do this before, and when he had cut a slice that was overthick, he paused and asked Wilkes whether it would do. I knew my great-aunt demanded crustless bread, as thinly pared as apple skin. I looked down at this assortment of cut bread, the thickness of mutton chops, with complete bemusement. Then I realized that my great-aunt's tray still stood in its place between the refrigerator and the larder, and that the tea now laid upon the table was just for us.

'Let's raid the larder,' my uncle said. 'What's humbug's favourite jam?' He opened the door and stood in its cool depths, the marble shelves above his head crammed with preserves and pickles kept especially for my great-aunt. He called to me, and I stood in the doorway muttering: 'I don't know, I haven't a favourite.' For I remembered once before, soon after I had arrived, he had asked me the same question. I had told him that I thought I liked apricot jam best, and he had answered then that it was a common taste, and said that they never had any. I had since had many opportunities to check the larder, and had found every variety of jam and pastes, many more than I knew existed, and some with names that

rang exotically, like tropical places in geography lessons. He had
supplied me then with plum jam, and that and fish paste was what
was generally served to me.

'I know,' he said excitedly, 'humbug is partial to apricot.'

I believe I ate a little of that jam then, but ever since I have
had a nausea for it. I had to smooth the dark thick orange syrup
upon the bread and nibble it slowly, for I was so sure my great-
aunt must be dead. It was not that fact which disturbed me, but
their strange behaviour. When Wilkes began to eat a slice of fruit
cake, she suddenly began to laugh again, sandy crumbs and spittle
spraying over the table; but my uncle's mood abruptly changed.
He frowned sternly at her then, nodding in my direction, placed
his finger to his lips.

Later we all heard my great-aunt's bell; it tinkled more slowly
than usual, but without saying a word, Wilkes rose from the table
and went upstairs.

One afternoon as we were all eating tea, we heard a sound from
the garden, and I saw that a young woman was about to enter the
conservatory. She walked through it as if she were quite at home,
then paused for a moment in the scullery, peering at the three of us.

Wilkes said: 'Well, if it isn't Alice.'

'Bin stayin' with me brother. Thought I'd just pop over and see
how you all are.' I didn't like the look of her at all. Her hair was a
bright yellow and frizzed out in two wings that hung awkwardly
just above her shoulders. I noticed that my uncle sat very still,
holding his tea-cup in the air. The woman smiled and murmured:
'Well, nothin's changed much around 'ere, 'as it?' Then she looked
at me and put her tongue inside her cheek. 'Well, quite the 'appy
family you look.'

Slowly my uncle placed his tea-cup back on its saucer, and then
he spoke for the first time, but not looking at the woman, looking
away at the kitchen door as if he wanted to escape. 'What is it you
want . . . Alice?'

'Mrs., now . . . Harper. Met me 'usband Fred in the army. 'E's
an electrician, we got a little flat, Brixton. But saving up we are,
want to buy a semi, bit further out. Too near the railway line we
are now. . . .'

'Have a cup of tea?' Wilkes said eagerly.

'Don't mind, ta.' She sat down, smoothed her floral print frock and sniffed, staring at my uncle half-amusedly, half-sneeringly. 'The years certainly 'aven't 'elped you, 'ave they, Woody? Maybe . . . well, it would be nice,' and she glanced at me, 'if we could 'ave a private chat, just the two of us, about old times, eh?'

My uncle began to stutter. 'I h-h-hardly think that's necessary.'

'Oh, you don't, do you?' she said loftily. 'Now, that's quite a laugh, seein' you all sitting pretty 'ere.'

He buttoned up his jacket, suddenly officious. 'Very well, Alice. Let's go into the drawing-room.'

She grinned and followed him out of the kitchen, leaving Wilkes and me alone. I had never heard anyone talk to my uncle in such a manner. It was very puzzling. 'I think, Wilkes, I shall go up to my room and read.'

'That's right,' Wilkes muttered, 'that's right, dear.' And she shook her head as if it was all bothering her as well. I hovered in the hall, taking refuge near the coat-stand. I could hear them whispering together, their voices hard, quick and urgent. Then she raised her voice.

'Bloody hell, it's not bleedin' much I'm askin'. . . .'

'I haven't got it, Alice.'

'Don't lie to me, you rotten sod, you an' your ma are bleedin' well sittin' on a gold mine. . . .'

'Most of the business I had to give over. It wasn't going well, you wouldn't understand . . . Well, you only have to look at the boards now. What does it say? – Willoughby, Pink & Sons. Doesn't that prove it?'

'Okay, then, if you want me to turn nasty. . . .', then she lowered her voice and I couldn't hear, but I heard my uncle cry out, whether from fear or disgust I couldn't tell. There was a long silence.

'I knew you'd help, Woody, yes I knew. . . .', then more whispering. I could hear my uncle moving about in the room, and then I heard her laugh. My uncle cursed her.

Perhaps it was after that when I returned from school that I found the house in an uproar. My uncle was arguing with a workman in the hall. At the same time I could hear my great-aunt upstairs calling out for help. Her door must have been wide open, for the sound she made, full of crudities and insults, could be clearly heard. Yet my uncle ignored that sound and went on arguing.

'That's what you're paid for, dammit.'

'I ain't got the tools, and that's the end of it,' the workman muttered sourly.

'It's worked before,' my uncle cried.

'It won't take the weight. If you leave it to the morning we can do the job then.'

'I've told you time and time again, it's urgent, it must be tonight.'

'Look, there's nothin' I can do.' And he turned to go.

My uncle had ignored me and I now took my hat and coat off and hung them up, as he took a wad of notes out of his pocket. 'I'll pay you. I will, look,' and he waved the money at the man. 'All you've got to do is go back home, get the tools and return here.' He started to peel off some notes and tried to hand them to the man.

I listened with interest to the sounds coming from upstairs.

'Great lumps of damned shit . . . you rotten devils. Help! You heathen buggers, I'll get yuh, all of yuh. Help!'

The workman turned away from my uncle and muttered: 'Some sods 'ave got more money than sense.' He left the house, slamming the door behind him. My uncle looked down at the money in his hand and swore. Then he glared at me. 'Trotter's the man,' he murmured and rushed down the hall and out into the back garden. I walked to the bottom of the stairs. There was no sound from Wilkes anywhere. I climbed the stairs softly, thinking that if the screen was in place I could pass my great-aunt's door without her seeing me, and so escape to my room. But as I reached the top of the stairs, I saw that the sounds did not come from her room at all. For the moment her fury was spent, and she was whimpering: 'Not a soul in the wide world loves yuh, what a poor sufferin' sad thing yuh are,' and she sniffed loudly. She was lying sprawled out upon the landing floor, her top half propped up by the wall. The turbulent golden array of her hair I now saw was a wig, for it had slipped sideways over one eye. She looked like a stranded circus elephant; her great breasts and belly were at the level of her nose, and her plump wrinkled ankles protruded from a froth of frilly lace like boiled pigs'-trotters on a bed of stewed apple. Above her, and blocking the stairs to the next floor and my haven, a wheel-chair swung lop-sidedly upon a rope, attached to a pulley on the wall. Next to this a large part of plaster had fallen away, revealing the brick beneath.

She looked up and saw me. 'Look, girl, look. On purpose. You're a witness, as the good Lord knows. On purpose.' I stood still, not knowing how I could flee from the obscene spectacle; she gestured to me to come close. 'Where's Bessie?' I shook my head. 'Where's Woody?' I shook my head again, for I was confused. 'There, so they've left me, all of 'em, is that it? Just you, eh?' She pointed to the chair. 'Bring it down.' I stared up at the odd piece of machinery, and wondered whether, if I dared touch it, the rest of the wall might fall down. 'Go on, yuh stupid little dunce,' she shrieked, 'pull the damn thing down.' I pulled at the chair; the pulley above whined, then moved, and the chair, quite easily, came to rest on the floor. 'Now, give me your hands.' I touched her for the first time; I felt her plump flesh damp with sweat, and it seemed as slimy as tripe. 'Pull me up,' she grunted. It was absurd. What was she dreaming of? I couldn't remotely budge her huge weight. I yanked, and she grunted, then I slipped and fell half on top of her. She screamed and swore at me, as my uncle and Mr. Trotter came running up the stairs.

Wilkes now appeared, framed in her bedroom door. Her eyes were red-rimmed and she still held a screwed handkerchief to her nose and sniffed loudly. Mr. Trotter stared up towards the attic. 'Up there and down again,' he muttered with disbelief. My uncle nodded grimly as my great-aunt mumbled more obscenities.

'Let's get you back into the chair then,' my uncle suddenly said, appearing to put a brave face upon the disaster. Mr. Trotter scratched the back of his head thoughtfully, then shook his head.

'No good adding to the labour, eh? What we need is a strong bit of canvas, roll her in it and then haul her aloft.'

My great-aunt's astonished outrage at this comment left her speechless for the first time; her head jolted forward like an angry turkey-cock, further dislodging the wig. Even I considered his remark rather odd, for I couldn't imagine there being a large piece of sail-cloth in the house.

'Son,' she murmured gently, 'it was not minutes ago when I heard the sweet sound of little Jenny Dove call.' She said the phrase with quiet command, but my uncle suddenly looked down at her with fear, and all colour drained away from his face. 'The chair,' she pointed, 'get me into the chair.'

My uncle at once bent down and tried to struggle alone with her weight. Mr. Trotter shook his head again, murmuring in general disbelief, then joined my uncle in his labour. I drew back and stood with Wilkes, as finally they heaved her into the wheel chair and step by step they lifted her up the stairs.

'Where's she going?' I whispered to Wilkes.

'Just to *the* room,' Wilkes whispered back, as if it were the most normal occurrence.

'The room that's locked? But why? What's in it?'

'Just a lot of old junk,' Wilkes muttered. 'Now don't you worry yourself.'

We heard the sound of the chair move along the landing above, then my uncle and Mr. Trotter appeared, both out of breath. 'How about a whisky, then? Come, that's the least I can do, Mr. Trotter. She'll be there for a while now, unless you'd rather go home?' My uncle paused. 'Downstairs, Emma, leave your great-aunt in peace.'

'May I stay with Wilkes?'

I should not have asked, for it hinted at our complicity, and immediately angered him. I was left alone in the kitchen. I believe they must have drunk a considerable amount of whisky, for their voices became quite loud, and at one point I thought they must be quarrelling; then Wilkes came down to prepare my great-aunt's supper tray. She shut the kitchen door and placed her finger to her lips, but I could not resist asking her questions. 'Why is the room locked? What's in it? Who's Jenny Dove, Wilkes? Why were you and uncle laughing so much that time?' She shook her head and would not say a word. 'Will you tell me next Sunday, will you, please?' She carved some cold ham, cut some bread and butter, then carried the tray to the door. She turned and gave me a little smile. 'That's just how his father used to laugh,' she nodded. 'Oh yes, just the same wild laugh.'

I heard them haul the wheelchair down the stairs, and Mr. Trotter stumbled through the kitchen. He stopped and looked at me, then winked and wagged his finger. 'I seen you lookin'. D'you like flowers then?'

'Very much. I think your garden. . . . I think it's lovely,' I ended lamely.

He came nearer and leant across the table. 'Yes,' he whispered. 'And it's mine and I won't have anyone touching it neither. Whatever they might say here. Don't you listen to them.'

I shook my head. 'No, I won't.' There was an awful intensity in what he said that frightened me. He was still leaning across the table staring at me. 'Mr. Trotter. . . . d'you know why my great-aunt went upstairs?'

'To look at her old self. It's vanity she's rotting away with, child.' Then he turned and went out through the garden, whistling.

I went upstairs to bed, undressed and hung my school uniform up in the cupboard. It was long and thin, built beneath the eaves of the roof, and I could see a chink of light in the darkness at the end. I climbed over some packing-cases, crouched on one and put my eye to the space. They had left the light still burning in the room, but my peephole disappointingly showed merely more suitcases. I worked at the hole with my fingers; it was lath and plaster which broke and crumbled away easily, so that in a matter of minutes I had made a hole as large as my hand where I could see most of the room.

It looked a little like Madame Tussaud's, though all the dummies were faceless. I recognized most of the costumes, for I had already seen them in the photographs. But even though they were covered in dust and were torn with age and neglect, there was something magical in their faded splendour; velvets and silks, nets and chiffons, sequins, tinsel and paste, frills, flounces. How stupidly dense I had been, not to connect Sadie with my great-aunt, for I could see now in her huge mask-like moon-face, the pert nose, shell-like ears, of that earlier coquette.

'But why does she go up there?' I asked Wilkes.

Wilkes frowned. 'Maybe she wants to remember how it all was.' She paused. 'Always happens after an upset . . . seems to comfort her.'

'Did you ever see her act?' I asked. 'How did she get so fat, and why can't she walk?'

'She's a law unto herself,' Wilkes muttered. 'And that's the end of it.'

This seemed most unhelpful. I decided to try another tactic. 'D'you hate her? I think my uncle is afraid of her.'

Wilkes shook her head doubtfully. 'I don't hate anyone. They all have a right to live and die as they wish.'

'Was she very famous? Did my grandfather love her very much?'

She nodded. 'Doted on her, nothing was too good for her, but always on the move she was, travellin' they were to foreign places, never could settle down, even when he came along. No, she wasn't the type to make a home, that upset Mr. Willoughby. Time and time again she left him, but he'd always take her back. Forgive her, he did, every time . . . oh my, I can tell you, the scenes I heard between them. Mind you . . . she was an actress all right, and I daresay could cry at will, but tear her clothing and such nice dresses she had, what a shame. Such violence you wouldn't believe, cutting her wrists and begging him to forgive her.' She paused. 'It was the war that did it, that brought on the change, gave everything up for him, she did, it was such a shock and a torment for her.'

'What was?'

She looked at me doubtfully, then shook her head. 'There's some things young children should never know.'

'Please, Wilkes . . . tell me,' I tugged at her sleeve.

'That's when she started to put on weight so. Oh dear me, she let herself go then, but fat or thin, he loved her. But she wouldn't act no more, nor go out either. So there it was. Two boys in the house, and him so spiteful to the babe, you'd have to watch young Norwood all the time, up to mean tricks he was, and there were times I wondered whether it wasn't her that put him up to them, close as two thieves they were at that time.'

I tugged again at her sleeve. 'You mean, the babe . . . was that my father?'

Then she gave me such a happy smile and nodded. 'That's right, Emma, and what a good child he was too. I can see him in you sometimes.'

'Those sure are mighty vicious killers,' my great-aunt murmured with pleasure as she stared up at Uncle Woody. 'Batterin' a whole family of happy holiday-makers to death with an axe. Well, maybe I should be thankful to the Good Lord that I can't stir from these shores. Have you read all about it, son?'

'No, Mother, you know . . . such things upset me.' My uncle clutched at his woollen cardigan as if he were suddenly cold. I had just finished the Bible readings and I was waiting to be dismissed. But my great-aunt was in a strange mood, irritable one moment and in the next making sinister comments about her spirit guide.

She sighed. 'Well, son, I think it does us all a power of good to read and know about all the violence in this wretched world. Now Woody, would you be capable of acting so murderously to people who just for one night stopped and camped on your bit of land?'

'I haven't read about it, Mother.'

'Well, I'm damn well tellin' yuh,' she shouted. 'Italian peasants, that's what they were, nothin' but peasants, and they just murdered this English family, aristocrats they were, cuz they trespassed. Jesus, it's a terrible world.' Then she threw me the Sunday paper and made me read out the whole story aloud.

Four years later when I ran from the house I remembered that story, and the smudged photographs of those other victims, for they echoed that senseless murder. I cannot see violets without feeling deep nausea. Oh my poor gentle Wilkes, I didn't wait to see you buried. Nor did I keep my promise to you, to place those trite little love verses you'd written thirty years before into your dead hands.

Rod

'There,' Emma pointed down. 'Just there, that's where she was.' We were in the tangled garden. 'What a vile-looking mess.' She was in an absurd mood: all gaiety one moment, then spiced with sudden resentful violence. She had screwed up a page of the *Guardian*, calling it 'tendentious *avant-garde* rubbish', and insisted we have a large glass of Chablis at ten-thirty in the morning. She kissed me briefly on the cheek. 'Roddy ducks, we ought to get out of it. Go away. Far away. To sun and sea and no bloody petrol fumes, telephones or trains.' She sat down beneath the broken glass of the conservatory, hugging her knees to her chin. 'That's it, to peace and serenity.' She turned and stared out again at the garden. 'And no violence,' she added softly. 'What's stopping us, eh? What's keeping us here? It can't be the past, which we both abhor and have rejected.'

'You're always running away.' I kicked a broken flowerpot. 'God, woman, you don't even know what from.' I thought of the way she worked only spasmodically on that book; her enthusiasm waned and would be replaced by despair.

'Yes I do. I'm running away from this house. But whoever it was that said run, also trapped me in a circle. . . .' She shrugged. 'So there, I run through the house, through the past, but again and again and again. . . .'

'Maybe if you just slowed down on your way through, just slowed up enough to get back what you lost . . . maybe then, you wouldn't have to come back.'

She held her glass up and stared at me through it. 'I hate you,' she said slowly. 'There's a profound discontent in you, Roddy boy, that sheds pessimism like a hound moulting.'

'That was supposed to be a hopeful remark,' I paused, trying to gauge her mood exactly. 'Look, Emma, I don't care. Let's go away, let's buy a jeep and ride off towards a huge desert so that we're immersed in nothing but sand and sun. . . .'

'And each other, and what we both know, always remember, can't forget. . . . D'you think a place like that would transform us, could change the fact that we both need and reject each other . . . ?'

'For fuck's sake . . . that's bloody absurd, and you know it.'

'How long have we known each other?'

I shook my head and drained my glass; she handed me hers and nodded to the kitchen to refill both. 'I don't mean a couple of years ago, when we first met. Not that I noticed you then.' She laughed. 'Well, that's what I'm getting at, the horror distinguished you. Before, you were anonymous. . . .'

I heard her voice go on and the sound of her uncle move slowly down the stairs above. What the hell did he do all day, locked up in his room? And if you crept past the landing you'd hear him, mumbling and chanting little verses like a bloody child. I returned and gave her both the bottle and the full glass.

'Six weeks,' she said, 'nearly . . . just counted it up.'

'Not very long,' I muttered.

'Six weeks, and you don't love me, oh no. . . .'

'That's ridiculous.' Her mood was making me angry.

'You just love the violence in me . . . no, that's not right; what excites you . . .' She was trying to find the right words, frowning and closing her eyes, searching her emotions. '. . . is the destruction, the blitz of my soul.' She nodded. 'That's right; Jumbo told me that Josie once said something to him. . . .'

'She never spoke to him in her life.'

'How the hell do I know? All I know is that Jumbo said that what terrified her was that maybe parents of children provoked . . .'

'Bloody well shut up,' I shouted. 'You've got it all wrong. If anyone said that, I said it to Jumbo.'

'Maybe she said it as well?'

'What? Use him as a confidant? For heaven's sake, Emma, Josie was a beastly snobbish prude. In her opinion dwarfs were uncivilized.'

'What on earth did you see in her then?' she said quietly.

I turned away and closed my eyes. God, what a time ago that was. I saw Josie's face against the context of her parents' cottage, filled with beastly little tombs to culture, collages of coloured postcards, memorials to visits abroad, fringed knick-knacks representing mock peasant handicrafts; ah yes, in that context she seemed fresh, blank, innocent. 'I can't tell you,' I murmured.

'Look, what was it in her,' she cried violently, 'what did she mean by what she said to Jumbo?'

'I don't know.'

'Can't you see why I ask you? I want to know if she attracted you in the way I do?' She was near me, staring up intently into my face.

'Look, Josie, let's not go on with this. . . .'

'What?'

'It's so self-destructive.'

'What did you call me then? You called me Josie. See? See what I mean?' She turned away. 'God, it doesn't matter what woman you sleep with, does it? We're all the bloody same, symbols of something.'

She went out into the garden, bending beneath a tree; then raising one slender arm, she hung to a branch, lifted both feet off the ground and swung gently. She was still a kid, I told myself, still a damned stupid irresponsible kid, not caring who or what she kicked. I heard her voice: 'Hi, Woody. What's it like in your cell up there? D'you want company?' I clung to her possessively; she drained me dry, empty; emotionless I still waited near her, hating every moment when I could not be in her company.

Then suddenly her arms were around me. I could feel her body pressed tightly to my back. 'Sorry,' she murmured, 'sorry, you are my love, you are, really.'

'If only. . . .'

'What?'

'If only, it wasn't just here, in this place. . . .'

She let go of me. 'Woody would hate it if I went away again.'

'Christ. You don't sleep with him.'

'No. Nor do I love him. Poor, poor Woody, how could anyone have loved him? Maybe that's why I came back, maybe that's why now I want to stay. Oh hell, let's open another bottle.'

I could hear her teasing him in the kitchen. 'Come on. have a glass, you old fraud. You know you drink up there. That's it. Let's all be friends together. Let's celebrate.' One of them dropped a glass. I looked down hazily at the empty bottles; there were only three. I felt deliciously drunk; the sun was up, the birds were

singing, not a cloud in the sky; maybe . . . yes, maybe I was a bit
hungry, but . . . Emma would make something later.

'You're a prejudiced narrow-minded old swine,' I heard her say,
'and you know it. What? Why do I think . . . ? What about those
gypsies, eh? And that great stinking fuss you made sending the
police scouring the countryside. . . .'

I walked into the kitchen, perfectly steadily I thought, but my
shoulder knocked against the door-jamb. Her uncle sat at the
kitchen table, a glass of wine at his side, polishing his spectacles
with a black-bordered handkerchief – highly suitable I thought for
his sombre persona. 'Tinkers, well known for snatching and pilfer-
ing,' he grumbled. His eyes blinked uncomfortably in the sunlight.

'What gypsies?' I asked.

'That's why I had the fence put up,' he went on, 'to stop them.'

'There was never any fence, you fuddled-headed old sod.'

'Course there was. A fence, a strong fence, you must have them.'

Emma shrugged and turned away, saying to me: 'He blamed the
murder on the gypsies. He told the police he saw them in Trotter's
garden. Now he says he didn't see them.' She laughed. 'Oh Woody,
my old darling, you mean you, the height of respectability, lied to
the police?'

He shook his head and muttered under his breath. 'It wasn't like
that at all. They came to our door. . . .'

'The gypsies?'

'Yes, the tinkers came to the door and I got rid of 'em, like
anyone would. Well, surely it was the most natural thing for them
to go round all the houses.' And he looked up at both of us, wanting confirmation.

'You change your story every time,' Emma said loftily. 'Now
you'll be telling me that Wilkes never picked the violets.'

'No. I did.'

Emma stopped drinking and slowly put her glass down, staring
down at the old man in disbelief.

The Parma violets: I almost smelt their scent in my mind; for it
was so pungent in Emma's horror when she had stumbled over the
thin bludgeoned body of the wan spinster in the tangled garden
that damp morning, unable to recognize the battered, splintered
face, but knowing too well the faded fawn clothes, tightly but-

toned upon the long body, now awkwardly turned as if all bones
had been savagely dislocated. I saw the child Emma turn in flight
and panic, making the soundless cry, run back through the house
to attempt some kind of clumsy entreaty from people who had
always rejected her.

'You picked them?' she said slowly.

'Yes, yes, it was all . . . her idea. . . .'

'Whose?'

'Oh dear me, yes, she was always full of pranks like that. . . .'

'You mean the old bitch . . . it was her idea?'

He laughed and looked up at me. 'Emma never took to her . . .
you know, not that many did. . . . Well, when she was younger
maybe.' He frowned. 'Yes, but Emma, you must understand, she
was old and ill, got bored, and . . .' he paused and tried to focus
on me, 'My mother was an actress you know, so she enjoyed little
dramas. . . .'

'Like murder,' Emma added bitterly.

'Well now, we were very shocked as you know. Poor mother
never got over that.'

'For God's sake,' Emma shouted, 'what the hell did she tell you
to do?'

'Pick them, pick Trotter's flowers.'

'But why?'

'Oh, I forget now,' he said anxiously. 'Wilkes had done something, oh, made mother cross, maybe confused her medicines or
pills. She did do that once I remember,' he said brightly, 'quite by
mistake, gave her some extra sleeping pills, instead of the iron
pills. Lord, she slept right through the day and well into the evening. How we did laugh when we knew. My word, I thought Wilkes
had killed her off.'

Emma's head was in her hands as the old man trailed off, chuckling; his eyes grew quite bright with nostalgia.

'So poor Bessie upset the great Saffron May Willoughby?'

He nodded. 'That's it, and she always hated Trotter, hated the
family, so she just planned to upset them both, that's all. She knew
his garden was sacrosanct, though it was ours really, so she suggested I pick some flowers and present them to Wilkes; they'd
have to be small so that she'd wear them. Then he'd see them, get

mad and shout at her.' He paused. 'It all seemed very harmless to us. The violets were the obvious choice; mind you, they were all under glass and a bit of a job to pick. But I got a nice big bunch and . . . well, I will say this, Wilkes was overjoyed. I said I knew Saffron was peeved with her, so I'd bought her these from the florist's to make up for it.'

I stared down at him; he seemed so complacent, so unaware. 'How bloody horrible.'

He darted a look at me. 'Yes it was. You're quite right. Horrible. But . . . well, you don't realize at the time.'

'Why the hell didn't you tell the police then?' Emma shouted.

'Saffron begged me not to. Besides . . . we still didn't think. . . . We hoped it couldn't have been Trotter. That's why I told them that I saw the gypsies.'

She shivered. 'He must have been mad anyway.'

'Voltaire suggests it's the ultimate sanity.'

'He didn't mean a real garden,' she snapped.

'Well no, but . . . maybe that's the only thing Trotter had.'

'It was.'

'So to violate that, would be like . . .' I couldn't finish the sentence.

'Yes, like murdering his child.'

Her uncle rose from the table and started to move out of the room, fumbling with his spectacles as he did so. She called out to him. 'So see what you've done. My God, if anyone ought to have murder on their conscience, it's you. Why the hell can't you feel for others? Why the damned hell haven't you ever imagined being inside somebody else's skin and thought of their vulner-ability?' She followed him shouting. 'You're wooden all through. If I'd been you I would never have had a moment's peace after that happened.' They disappeared into the hall. I heard him mumble something; he sounded so childish, so pathetic; was he trying to apologize? I followed them. They were standing at the bottom of the stairs.

Suddenly she struck him across the face with such fierceness that his spectacles flew off hitting the wall. 'I loathe you,' she screamed. 'Why the hell don't you die? Go on, die.' Then she turned, walked down the hall and out of the front door; he bent down and crouching on the floor tried to feel for the spectacles. I went over to him and picked them up, then put them into his hand. He was sobbing like a small child, gulping for air, his thin chest jerking, his tiny red eyes streaming with tears.

'B-b-b-badly?'

'One glass cracked and the frame's broken in the middle. Maybe I could stick it together with a bit of plaster.'

'Could you?'

I put my arm around him, and with a sigh he leant his head upon my shoulder. 'Come on now, I'll help you upstairs. She didn't mean all that. Don't let her upset you.' Slowly we climbed the stairs, and slowly his sobbing stopped; how strange, I thought, it was as if I was comforting Lucy in a nightmare, this feeble-headed old man full of a great gulf of anguish, his body almost as frail as the daughter I once had. 'You must have another pair, eh? Surely?'

'But . . . how can I find them?' He paused at the top of the stairs and sighed. 'Can't remember where I put them. But . . .' he sobbed again and shook his head. 'It's all true. True. But I never intended any harm. D'you understand?'

'Yes, I understand.'

'Do you? Would everyone believe that? Never . . . never intended what happened.' He fumbled and put the spectacles on; they went crooked, making him look like a misshapen owl. He stood outside the door of his room.

'Will you be all right?'

He took a key out of his pocket. 'Thank you, sir. Thank you,' he murmured. I realized he was waiting for me to leave before he opened the door.

I turned away, then hesitated as I heard his voice again. 'Yes, yes, of course, Emma's quite right. There couldn't have been a fence then, for how could I have picked the violets?'

Part Two

Confession

Trigger

'So you don't bleedin' fancy 'im then?' I'm lying on the bed, watching her. She yowls like a tom pussy scratching and pissing love-spray.

'Course I don't flamin' fancy 'im. 'E's good for a fiver, ain't 'e?'

''Ow do you pose then? Show me.'

'In my black lace knickers, that's 'ow.'

'What, them? They're no bigger than a bleedin' powder puff.'

She picks 'em up, swings 'em from their ribbon like a poovy angel boy's censer, then wriggles 'er top so that 'er tits jiggle. 'Cor, Trigger,' she says, 'I don't 'alf like it when you're jealous. 'Ere,' she says, 'would you be flamin' mad if I went with 'im then? Want to throttle 'im, eh?'

I grab both 'er tits and screw 'em hard, so she goes mad and shrieks. 'I'd take a razor to you, lovey gal, yeah, first.'

She lies panting across the bed.

'That is,' I said, 'if you didn't 'ave four of 'em fivers stuffed in yer 'andbag.' I let 'er go. 'Cos that's the lowest price your flamin' pussy's worth.'

'I love you, Trigger,' she says, all meek as milk, and I bend over 'er, me tongue glidin' like a snake 'neath her tits; gorgeous she is, breasts 'eavenly plump on ribs you can play on, so that me juice begins to pump and I 'ave to stop, cos I don't want me leather trous to stink. I shove 'er away, an' up she gets all mean with her thundery-bitch look.

''Ere,' she says, ''ow about you bringin' back some loot, eh? 'Oo's the fuckin' breadwinner around 'ere, I'd like to know, eh?' An' she bends down and puts that frilly pouch on that covers her fan, then purrs an' strokes 'er tits.

'Workin' on a job, I am.'

'Oh yeah, who with?'

'I got connections. We gotta wait for a bit, that's all.'

Sadie puts 'er pink trous on and dolls 'erself up like a film star.

''Ow long does this bleedin' artist chap think this joke's goin' on for, then?'

''Ow the 'ell do I know, Trigger? Last time 'e said someink abart me stayin' this weekend.'

'What? At 'is place?'

She shrugged. 'Yeah, where else? Cos the 'tecs want to catch us in bed or someink.'

'Bleedin' well on the job, you mean?'

She pins up 'er 'air. 'You're bleedin' mad. 'E's flamin' queer, you know that.'

'Well, 'e's married now, ain't 'e? 'E's got a kid, ain't 'e?'

'Yeah, and so 'ave you. So what?' She bends down, picks up her 'andbag. 'Anyways, I said to 'im, it's not on, cos I can't leave Trigger, not for a 'ole night.' She bends over, kisses me, then ruffles me 'air. 'Cor Jesus, you're a flamin' good-looker, and that's the truth, Trigger. I love yer, you know that.'

She leaves, bangin' the door. 'Okay, if 'e wants this weekend, screw 'im, Sadie.'

She opens the door again. 'Course I could ask 'im,' and she goes all coy, 'maybe 'e'd fancy an exhibition, just the two of us, eh, Trigger? What abart that?'

'You damn well know I don't do nothin' dirty. What we do, Sadie, together is personal.' Then I'm shoutin'. 'You fuckin' slut, you know that.' She runs, shit-scared.

I'm fuckin' fed up. Chew me knuckles raw. I don't even 'ave the lol to buy the gas for the fuckin' motorbike. Rod's told me what the bleedin' fuzz said, and that's one thing I'm not goin' to do. Okay, I'm sex crazy for Sadie, but I've always bin protective to my birds, look after 'em proper, give 'em great times, 'ave wads of fivers to spend, and 'ere we are stuck in one bleedin' room. Whatsa matta with you, Trigger? You King of the Dykes or not? I stare at meself in the lookin' glass. There must be somethin' in this stinkin' sewer of a town where Trigger me boy could get some loot without the fuzz knowin'. Breakin' and grabbin's too chancy unless I move on

and out, but Jesus, my roots're in this stinkin' place. I've me kid
which me Mum looks after, except at weekends when 'e stays with
Sadie an' me. I love that kid. Yeah I know what Rod feels; if any
fuckin' swine mucked with my kid I'd cut 'is balls out an' ram 'em
darn the swine's throat. That's what I call perversion. The fuckin'
men that do that should be torn apart; the fuzz oughta torture
'em like what the nazis did to the bleedin' jews, that might put a
stop to it. Yeah, but the fuzz 'ave gone soft now. Why the fuckin'
'ell shouldn't I get some loot out of them rich jews? They made
it, didn't they, stealin' it from poor buggers with their spongin' an'
cheatin' – all called big business – over-fuckin'-chargin' us poor
bleeders . . . yeah, all I did was try and even it out a bit. But fuck
it, all they want to do is put me back inside, lock me up for life,
instead of findin' that swine 'oo killed poor Rod's kid. They didn't
even find that one before, down the street from me, when I was
a kid, what the 'ell was 'er bleedin' name? Like a fuckin' bird or
somethin'. Dove. That was it. Jenny Dove, she played with me, but
'er ma was a snot-nosed prig; off the poor little bleeder gets sent
to some posh school, and there, didn't that prove somethin'? Got
done in be'ind the bushes off Ditchling Road, last seen wearin' 'er
baby pink that she was so fuckin' proud of, showin' off to us rough
lot that never saw one new dress from one year to the other, all
bleedin' net it was like a flamin' tea-cosy. Cor fuck me if she didn't
'ave 'er comeuppance.

'Sadie's late,' Jumbo grins, runnin' 'is spongy tongue 'cross
blubber lips.

'She's on a job.'

'What job, Trigger?'

I empties the pint – sour fuckin' beer it was. 'Some bleedin'
poove. 'Is wife sets the 'tecs on 'em both, knowin' it's all a put-up
job, and the 'tecs are so bleedin' stupid they keep on losin' 'em.
Why the fuck should Sadie care? She gets a tenner a time.'

'Tenner, eh? Is he rich?'

The thick little fucker isn't even lookin' at me. 'Is pudgy
fingers're fiddlin' at 'is belt, starin' at the door. Rod's bird's just
come in, and quick as fuckin' lightnin' Jumbo 'as an 'ard on, bulgin'
like a bleedin' truncheon.

'Dun' you stick that whopper near me, you filthy fucker, or I'll bleedin' cut it off. Give it the karate chop.' 'E darts me a' evil stare an' runs off back, carryin' 'is cockload like a prize marra stuffed wid dynamite. I see the bird look after 'im, kind of appealin' . . . maybe she could do with 'is filthy thing. Some of them wizened whores a 'undred years old 'ad 'im crazy, but then their quims're as 'uge an' slack as carrier bags an' sailors with bleedin' little courgettes're as much use to 'em as a vicar's sneeze. Jumbo vanishes to flog 'is 'ampton, tho' 'ow 'e gets 'is fist round it, maybe 'e does a bit of spit an' polish and the pansies in the piss 'ouse 'ave a pull too.

No wonder the ugly bugger got stiff. Why the 'ell does she come 'ere anyway? All alone tonight. Funny. Got style, she 'as. Expensive clothes. Smells good too. The colour of peach; 'air, skin, tight silky arse. . . . Cor, wonder whether she ever 'ad 'er clit tickled? Must 'ave at 'er bleedin' public school. Bet I could make 'er. Yeah, if I played it cool. Get 'er boozed up. Yeah, but that kind of stylish bird only sips bloody pink bubbly. What the 'ell do I care? Money. Fuckin' money. I need some loot. She's got money. Must 'ave. Couldn't wear clothes like that. She goes through the bar all the time movin', never seen that baby still. . . . Jesus, she's got legs . . . what legs. Why the 'ell does she keep on movin' . . . ? Emma Willoughby. Some name! What does she see in a bum like Rod? Back out she goes, searchin' the bars again. Bet she's a nympho . . . bet 'er pussy's white-'ot. Jesus, I'll kill Sadie, keepin' me waitin', no bird keeps me waitin' just cos I'm bleedin' skint. Fuck Sadie. I foller the bird. She goes 'cross the beach, walks near the sea.

'Hi Trigger, you look sad.'

She sits by me. I smell peaches, maybe limes . . . yeah, or lemons. Wish I could speak, can't say nothin', wish I could touch 'er. Don't dare. Bet she never wants a woman. Bet she's piss-scared of bein' touched by a woman. Bet she's a prick-sucker, an' if I brought out the old rubber dong, its 'ead all aglow with face-cream an' whacked 'er arse and crack, she'd never let on that she wanted more. Christ, what the 'ell do women want t'be male-lovers for? All that putrid stench, all awallow in grease an' sweat . . . cor makes me puke.

'Why did Jumbo run away?' she says, 'Doesn't he like me?'

I don't tell 'er 'e's got a letch for 'er same as bleedin' mount Etna eruptin'. 'We ain't seen Rod around lately. We ain't seen 'im, an'

I s'pose Jumbo's sore, see, cos we all were workin' for Rod, in a manner of speakin'.'

'Working?' she says.

'Yeah, all of us, on that job we were. Cos the police don't do no good, do they? Don't find no child-murderers, do they? They're no good, an' Rod, see, use' to pay us. Paid us all, well, for information, see.' She don't take the bait. She says nothin', looks away at the sea rollin' in. 'What you thinkin'?'

'Nothing much.' She sighs. 'Oh, just some stupid old cow covered in jewels.' She don't say no more.

' 'Oo was that, then?'

She shakes her head. 'Look, Trigger, here's some money.' She stuffs notes in me hand. 'Give some to Jumbo.' She gets up. 'I don't want the bloody stuff. And tell Jumbo, yes, tell him to come up and see us. He knows the house. He's been there before.'

'Okay, Jumbo, give. Why the secret? We can all see the bird 'as got style? It's a fair swop. I give you the message.'

'What she say to you. Tell me again.'

Crouched on the beach we are, everythin' stinkin' of tar an' salt an' the night as close an' black as a solitary.

'She wants you.'

'Why can't she tell me herself?'

'Cos she's scared stiff of Rod an' she came special tonight, see, but cos you ran off she thought you got the hate itch for 'er, see. Besides, you ain't easy for a bird like that to speak to. She got me, I'm a go-between, see.'

'It don't sound right, Trigger.'

'It don't sound right cos it's what you want, Jumbo. Cos I know and that bird knows that you 'aven't sniffed even at those tarts' old prunes since you first set eyes on 'er.'

Jesus, the dumb bleedin' little ogre's bein' fuckin' difficult. What am I doin' but givin' the ugly gin-drunk dwarf a princess on a plate, an' 'e sits on 'is small arse an' does nothin' but sucks in 'is great lips and snorts like a flamin' racehorse. 'Tell it to me slow,' he says, 'with all the details. Don't forget nothin',' he says.

'Okay. She comes over to me. I buy 'er a drink.'

'What?'

'Christ, *you* know what she drinks. It was . . . red, sticky.'

He shakes his head. 'She don't drink anythin' red an' sticky.'

'Tonight she does. Tonight she just fancied somethin' like that. . . .'

'She must be feelin' low,' the dumb oaf mutters.

'Course she was, cos you ran off and wanked yer big prick.'

'She didn't know that.'

'No. Birds with class don't 'ave orgasms in piss 'oles. So she says to me that Rod . . . well, he don't serve her like she wants. Besides the poor sod's sick, ever since 'is kid got done in 'e can't get a 'ard on. Then she says, look Trigger, my mum left me a lot of junk, you know, classy jewels an' suchlike, an' she don't wear the stuff cos she ain't like that. Bring Jumbo, she says. I want Jumbo, she says. He know's 'er 'ouse, she says.'

'Yeah, I been there.'

'So she's a bird with money, so she wants us to 'ave it.'

'You wanna break in?'

'She's itchin' to get 'er 'ands on you, Jumbo. It's simple. You've seen our Roddy in 'ere pissed as arse-'oles tonight. I'll tell Lulu to get 'er mad matelots to rough 'im up, then one of Lulu's birds takes 'im back to 'er place. That's Roddy fucked up for the night.'

'Maybe,' he says slow-like, 'maybe she does want me.'

''Aven't I bin sayin' so?'

He takes a gulp of gin from the bottle he keeps in 'is bum pocket: all the left-overs, the mucky dregs the sods left.

'So,' he says, 'why break in. Why you, eh?'

''Aven't I told yer?'

'No,' he says.

Bloody 'ell, s'pose 'e's right? I just thought 'e'd charge up there in a bull-rage and batter the bloody front door down and get on with the job while I 'as a good look-see. So I go grand an' with a bit of special mystery, I say: 'Cos that makes 'er quim 'ot. Cor, Jumbo lad, you know these eddicated birds only get going when you do the old dramatics. They like their sex decorated like a flamin' Christmas tree. Nothin' wrong with that. Sadie, the other day, 'ad this bloke callin' 'imself Robes-spear, the dumb slut thought 'e was some cousin of Shakes-speare, anyway she 'ad to pretend to cut 'is 'ead off. So maybe Rod's bird wants us to break in an' steal 'er ma's jewels cos she don't like 'er ma. . . .'

It don't matter what I say. I know 'e'll do it. I could go on all night chattin' 'im up an' saying what I bleedin' like an' 'e'd still be playin' Charlie Laughton a-cacklin' on the cathedral bells with 'is red tongue slobberin'.

The fuckin' 'ouse's barred up like a bleedin' prison. We tries all the downstairs windows. Not a light on anywhere, quiet as a grave. 'Shin up a fir tree, Jumbo.' Go on, like a bleedin' Christmas fairy. Cor, it's a burglar's bleedin' paradise. Trees everywhere, great thick branches scrapin' the walls an' upstairs windows. What they do in there for air? Must all suffocate. The poor sods, not even a bloody fanlight open.

'Well, get on the bloody roof can't you?' Thought you were in the circus. Blimey, with legs like fuckin' aubergines, no wonder you flopped. See. Now that's real knowhow. In 'ouses like this there's always a skylight, with huge empty attics an' never a soul to know if you stick yer bloody fist right through the glass.

'Take the torch, you stupid sod.' I kick the glass in with my boot. It shatters and falls. A fuckin' tom-cat yowls. Yeah, just the same noise that Sadie makes when she comes. Well, 'ere goes, I'll fuckin' show 'er. With a bit of luck I'll make enough to last a month or two an' she'll live it up like a duchess.

I drop into the attic and catch Jumbo. I shine the torch around.

'Christ. What the fuckin' 'ell?'

Jumbo lets out a shriek of fright. I kick 'im.

'It's bloody Tussaud's.' I find the light and switch it on. Nothin' but bloody dress-maker's dummies done up in fancy clothes, 'cept the clothes are all torn an' filthy an' covered in muck an' dust. I try the door. Locked.

'Bloody 'ell.' If we bust that it'll wake 'em. I shine the torch round. 'Look at that, Jumbo, even bloody kids, done up all fancy.' How many? Two, three, all girls, with cloth faces an' glass hat-pin eyes. Then I bend down and open a small chest. Filled with jewels, all bloody paste by the look of 'em, showy like the stuff they 'ave in pantos.

''Ere,' Jumbo says. 'Thought she wanted us to break the door down.'

'Subtle,' I say. 'Ya gotta be subtle. No good proper terrifyin' 'er.'

'E peers about, picks up a damned kid's dummy an' hugs it, doin' a flamin' dance. Then I see a 'ole in the wall as big as a kid's 'ead an' bash it in, shine the torch through. Seems to be a cupboard, so I shoves Jumbo in with the torch, an' 'e goes through an' puts anuvver light on. I follow. The wall breaks like fuckin' paper. This door ain't locked. There's a landin' an' we creep down stairs that bloody creak like piglets. Doors, doors, doors, I get fuckin' bored an' start switchin' lights on all over the bloody place. Jumbo runs about like a bitch on 'eat. Big white room, fuckin' empty. Whole fuckin' 'ouse empty. What did I say? Fuckin' burglar's 'eaven? Spend the whole night 'ere and turn the fuckin' place upside-down, 'cept Jumbo starts whinin' an' callin' the bird's name. 'Well, it's not my bleedin' fault,' I says, 'if she don't keep 'er promises. You an' I,' I say, 'we'll just hang about, see? She'll come back.'

Anuvver door locked opposite the big white room. I shake it. Come back to that later. So I starts the system. Do the desk first. All drawers turned upside-down. Bit of loose cash. Couple of notes. Nothin' there much. Do the kitchen. Nothin'. Couple of silver candlesticks in the dinin'-room. Pity. Too fuckin' bulky.

Then Jumbo comes doin' 'is party trick.

'What the bleedin' 'ell 'ave you got on?'

'She might fancy me in drag,' he says, grinnin' like a fuckin' chimp.

'You look bleedin' like a 'orror film,' I tells 'im. Done up in pink net with a fuckin' coronet of bloody daisies stuck on 'is 'ead. We go up the stairs an' I do the big white room. Few more notes lyin' on the dressin' table, an' Jumbo dancin' about on 'er bed singin' fuckin' nursery rhymes, when this old bloke suddenly turns up, standing there in 'is pyjamas, starin' at Jumbo and lettin' out a shriek like a fuckin' maniac dingin' onto the door. Cos we just stay still an' stare, then Jumbo jumps off the bed an' dances more but the bloke goes on screamin' an' tries to run but I gives 'im a knock on 'is 'ead so 'e goes down flat on the floor an' I just 'opes I 'aven't done 'im in.

Then I stares at Jumbo an' it all clicks. Bang. Wham. Back as a kid I am watchin' li'el Jenny Dove in 'er new dance frock on 'er toes in front of our row of council 'oushes. Trigger, I says to meself, you bleedin' well 'ad a break. You're in for the big time, boy. Cor.

Woody

This room of mine . . . yes, at times it seemed secure. It clothed me, was the armour I needed; at the best of times it gave me pleasure, with gaily clothed puppets hanging from their strings above the tiny stage of my theatre. The best times were when I could play with these, losing myself completely in their lives, so different from my own, these painted dolls with their mechanical limbs and wide-eyed expressions frozen in joy. I liked the way they gently swayed; at least I knew they were at peace; and when I became them, involved in their actions, I too felt something akin to peace. Though I wonder if there is a human being that exists who has found it and remained within it? Some say this is what God is. But Saffron's God was merely an exaggeration of her own thirst for vengeance. In the Bible itself there is no peace, and other works of piety I have read contain merely the hunger and search for peace, but never the attainment. I know what they all say; there are certain key phrases that are repeated by the saints and contemplatives, such as 'that the peace of God is within you', and that 'to love others with truth and infinite compassion above all else is to finally gain that blessed serenity'. Both of these measures I tried, knowing that my path would be arduous and maybe endless. Did I not show Saffron all the patient concern of a loyal son? Bearing her taunts, her scorn, the vindictive power she possessed over me, never allowing me to be free of the guilt that deformed me, with Stoic rectitude? What was the use? She and I drew violence to us, like lame beggars, hosts of parasites.

Wasn't I terrified of having the child live with us? Didn't I beg and plead with her, my mind contorted with the grotesque fear of those monstrous feelings that might at any time flame up? But since the moment Wilkes came to her, whimpering like a beaten dog, over the orphan child that Thomas had spawned, Saffron swelled with secret triumph; her mind teemed with plans, to use the child, subjugating me, humiliating me, making her a symbol of both my crime and my desire. She saw me lost in an orgy of terror and longing, and wanted to indulge her senses in that feast.

But Emma never knew how precious she was to me. How I longed to make friends, to draw her out, away from her fear which isolated her and gave her the semblance of someone much older. She wore a mask for all of us, carefully wrought, with a painted adult stare, but I sensed and loved the child beneath. Yet I did not dare to make contact, for though there was something about her of the same free innocence that Josie had, how could I be certain that what I thought and felt would not crumble away and leave just the raw naked sensation, the frenzy of physical fulfilment which at the time drowned everything else? Besides, any friendship, however pure, with Emma, would have given Saffron too much pleasure. My war with my mother was more powerfully significant. But I was jealous of Wilkes, and the way they grew close, spying and hating both of us. So when she was killed . . . yes, oh yes . . . I did hold Emma in my arms then, and tried, oh, how I tried, to contain all the panic and horror . . . holding her struggling body tight to me and crying with her. But it's too late . . . everything, always too late, to construct one gesture that is considered by the world as good, out of the emptiness and former despair . . . it is too late and Emma wants me to die.

I do not know how to die. I have sat here, sitting in that same armchair that Saffron sat in when I was ill as a boy – all that is tangible of that myth – and wondered how I should die. I have thought of the ways other people have killed themselves: those pills, razor blades, gas taps . . . all, I daresay, would do the job, and another human shred of skin and bone would be erased. I feel no fear at that final extinction. I welcome the thought. What stops me? Why do I sit here hesitating still, long into this night? Is it the strange knowledge that something would not have been finished by my death? That whatever caused the crime goes on independent of me, and I long to understand what it is? If only I could explain. Tell it all. As it was. Not ask for mercy nor forgiveness, but within me I beg, plead for a shred of understanding.

I sit in the empty house alone. Then I go to the toy theatre and pull the red velvet curtains across. I shall undress. I shall lie on my

bed in the dark. I shall eat no food nor drink even water. I shall lie
. . . as if asleep, remote. But my mind is full of whispers. Those
ghosts with devil limbs curse, cry and mouth obscenities.

I see clearly in the dark the image of a sword, with a bright silver
blade flashing, slice across my eyes; then I see the eyeballs, great
globular grass-green spheres, slashed by a river of scarlet. The
sound of shattered glass. Footsteps above, hushed voices murmuring . . . oh God, have mercy . . . Lord hear me . . . those dark shades
of evil dressed in her fine rags have risen up into malevolent life and
now are moving through the locked room. Cage them tight. Good
Lord, strike them dead. Kill, sweet Lord, that cursed woman.

No, this is not so. I am awake still within a nightmare. There
are no sounds. They are all inside my head. If I sit up, if I control
myself, they will go quiet. With my will I can silence them. Where
are my spectacles? Where did I put them? Where is the light?
Where is the table by my bed? The spectacles were on it. Damn
those noises. They are still there, getting louder . . . coming out of
the room. I can hear them on the stairs. Oh, good Lord, 'tis nothing . . . Emma, that's all. How could I forget Emma? She's back.
But why did I not hear her before? Why did the noises begin up
there? In that room above? I was asleep. I must have been asleep.
She woke me. Call out to her. Open your mouth. There, you can't.
No sound. You try and try to call her name, there's no sound. Then
you still must be asleep. Yes, that's it. That's why you can't find the
table. That's why nothing is where it is. See if you can see the light
of the street-lamp through the curtains. There you are, nothing,
no light, all is in darkness, pitch-black vile darkness.

No. Not Emma. I know her steps, not the man either. So that
proves again I'm locked in a nightmare which mocks me as if I'm
awake. Curious steps, one a little hushed, as slithery as a panther;
and the other . . . yes, heavier, rumbling with a discordant rhythm
. . . a hop, then flat and pouncing, like a drunk sailor trying to keep
his balance in a storm. But it's all in my head. No, no, they try the
door, they shake my door. A voice . . . it's no man nor woman
either . . . curses. Oh God, now what's that noise? Like a child
whimpering and whining calling Emma's name . . . it goes on and
on . . . with a shuffling limping sound and doors banging . . . will
it never stop?

This sheet wound tight about me, this blanket above and the quilt . . . yes, the quilt has a tear in it . . . there, just there. I can feel the soft feathers. Saffron's hats. Hundreds of her tiny hats. Now, which wall is that? With my fingers I follow the wall, stretching out my arm. It reaches a corner. There, below it, is the bolster . . . no pillow? But the other side of the bolster there must be the table . . . with the lamp and the spectacles. Yes . . . see, you just need to be calm. The sounds are distant now, far below . . . not in the house at all. They can't be. They never existed outside your mind. Now, the lamp. Thank God. Light. There, the spectacles in your hand. Now put them on. Look about you. See? No sounds. You're awake now. You did have a nightmare, you stupid old man, because the pillows are on the floor and you must have woken up the other side of the bed. So get up. Make the bed. Open the door. Look outside. Reassure yourself. No, I'm afraid. Look at you, your hands are shaking. Shush. Noises again, oh dear God. It must be Emma. Listen. Listen carefully . . . yes of course, the silly girl is drunk, she's singing . . . old nursery rhymes. That's it, open the door, unlock it, peer round it, see? All the lights are on. Emma's door is wide open. . . .

Devils. Not Jenny Dove. Devils.

Pain. Fierce burning pain like a white-hot poker slashed across my scalp. Blackness. Open eyes. There, you can see . . . ceiling paper frayed . . . yellow ring of old damp, had the gutter mended year after the war. A man. Police. Thank God. Confession. A man. Searching. No, a boy in black leather studded jacket emptying drawers. Stopping. Coming over, staring down at me.

'You okay?'

'Who are you?'

'You and me gotta talk, we 'ave.' Then he shouted, ''Ere, Jumbo, stop larkin' and get a glass of brandy for the old bloke, otherwise 'e's goin' to die on us.' He shook his head. 'Cor, awful colour you are, mate. I didn't 'it you 'ard either. A playful tap, that was.'

'I've got no money, I'm a poor man.'

'Shut yer gob. You got plenty. Look.' He took out of his pocket the notes I kept in my handkerchief drawer and waved them in front of me. 'That'll do for goin' on with. It's the continuin' supply

I'm interested in, see?' Then he shouts again. 'What's keepin' you, Jumbo?'

'I'll call the police.' I tried to make it sound strong, but I could hear my voice shake with nervousness, and he just laughed.

'Yeah, nice joke that would be, wouldn't it? Police be interested in you, wouldn't they?'

'Don't know what you mean.'

'Don't yer?' He just smiled, then cocked his head on one side, listening. 'I'm a muvver you know, yeah, I got a li'el kid, he's four . . . don't interest you at that age, do they? Cor, what you look so alarmed about. You play right with me, mate, and we'll both be livin' cushy.' He grinned again and ran his hand through the tight blond curls of his hair. He was a devil . . . neither male nor female, but in a terrible way, beautiful . . . oh yes, his face was classical, sharply incisive. 'Ah, 'ere's our dolly servant gal with the booze.'

I was screaming in terror again, shrieking and screaming and trying to run away and out of the room, run from the sight, as they laughed and danced and pulled me back, shoving me on to the bed, and the man or whatever she was, held me down as that thing poured the brandy down over my face and eyes, and the spirit stung my throat that was still screaming, though what sounds there were were now but the choking of someone who only desired to die and be defaced from sight and sound.

'He dun like yer face, Jumbo. You gives 'im the shit frights. Poor bleeder. Do we make you suffer, eh? Cor, dear me . . . there, I forgot, Jumbo, you got newly christened tonight . . . yeah, you're called Miss Jenny Dove.'

Both of them sat down and stared at me. Waiting. Just the three of us, waiting.

'Dunno what you think, Trigger, but he looks half dead to me.'

'Dear me, we don't want that. A nasty 'eart attack wouldn't be at all a good thing. I think . . . er, Miss Dove, if you'd be so kind as to leave us alone and go on clearin' the mess up, make it all tidy see, cos I think seein' you near 'im might upset 'is ticker.'

He, she . . . the one they call Trigger, sat down again and stared, then he lit a cheroot and puffed at it slowly.

'Okay, Mr. Willoughby, let's do business. My price is . . .' he flicked his ash on the rug, '. . . five hundred nicker per month in advance in cash. How does that strike you?'

I took the bottle of brandy and gulped at it. It helped. The fire of it seemed to give me some strength. 'Mad,' I heard myself say. 'You're quite mad. Whatever for? This is blackmail, it's absurd. What have I ever done?'

'I knew Jenny . . . yeah . . . twenty-five years ago. That's when I last saw that dress, too. You did the others in too, didn't you? You're kinky for bleedin' dancin' girls, look.' He picked up some ribbons and threw them in my face. I looked down at the floor and saw the crumpled dresses, the voile and net, the pink and blue spotted one; who had worn that? No, some of them . . . I never knew their names. I never read about it in the papers afterwards.

Perhaps this night of terror was what I had waited for? Perhaps I could explain to this creature why and how it all happened? I began to speak. But he spat and struck at me, like Emma, shouting obscenities and filth.

It was a long time before they left. I promised them everything. The money seemed unimportant, if only they'd leave me in peace. But Emma hadn't come back. I was afraid she'd gone again, and this time forever, and I should be left alone in this house. All the next day I waited and listened for her return.

Then suddenly I felt a torment of fury, a great surge of violence that flooded through me against everything that created my wretched life. I stole quietly down into the conservatory and picked up the axe lying there, then went upstairs to Saffron's room, of sacred memories.

The vile faceless dummies stare back at me. I hit at them with the axe, wildly, and as each one falls and splinters, I feel an enormous joy and relief. I lose all sense of time and place. I am destroying her. At long last I am killing Saffron May and she lies in filth beneath my feet.

Emma

I was sitting on the top deck of a green bus. The trees, thick with foliage, scraped the windows, and between the trees I could see the large bourgeois houses, individually styled, all hideous, in absurd mockery of the past. What I abhorred was not that I'd struck him . . . I didn't care a damn, I'd like to do it again and again. . . . No, what made me sit here, insulated in loathing, was the fact that he'd brought my own past so sharply back. Images shot forward, as bright and clear as coloured slide projections, the sound track behind them a turbulent murmur of hysterical whispers: that séance Saffron gave, when I had hidden behind the screen listening to her silly rubbish, until I had felt that there was something too real and horrid in my uncle's reactions. The bus stopped. There was the Spanish house, its tiny balconies crowded with scarlet geraniums. Then the time Wilkes had shown me my father's old letters and postcards, scribbled from all over the world; she had wept a little, then given them all to me. I knew every one off by heart. I saw through his eyes all those places: Gibraltar, Cairo, Aden, Hong Kong, Singapore. Wilkes' own life was full of people she loved and had loved; in her frailty she had been able to give love strongly. Now bitterly, how I wished she had taught me that quality.

At the top of Dyke Road I got off the bus, walked across the crest of the hill and on to the Downs. The wind was high, shifting large white clouds in huge puffed patterns over the humped hills, bending the seeded grass in sudden serpentine shapes that would be erased as soon as they appeared. I breathed the air, and hoped its salt-laced purity would scrub clean the soul's memories.

Why the damned hell did I allow this thing with Rod to go on? Was it just a great sorrow I felt for a man who had lost a child and grown mad with that anguish? And that obsessive search; he had to find out who had murdered the child and why this search that went in strange phases, now freeing him when we became lost in each other, then descending down over him, so that he'd go back to that bar, to those contacts who merely used his pain for their own mercenary ends; or spend a day in the library, re-reading old copies of *The Times* that recounted other cases of child assault, hoping to find some similarities; did I find all that merely pathetic, a madness that would fade; or so profoundly real to him that only when he found the man, and perhaps understood him, would he find that uneasy peace? But why the hell should I be part of it? Drawn into a search that must be for me only a grotesque fantasy?

Suddenly I remembered . . . ah, yes, how odd, that conversation with Josie. Why on earth? Wasn't that particularly strange that we discussed . . . ? I lay down in the long grass.

The child . . . Lucy was playing in that place opposite Park Crescent. Josie and I, each of us, were on a swing, just slightly moving it to and fro, watching Lucy as she rode the turnstile, while other children, who were older, scruffier, pushed it round. That afternoon seems in my memory to be all white. Perhaps it was the brilliant sunshine? Or that . . . by some chance, we all wore white. Josie and I . . . we didn't look at each other, we were staring at Lucy. Josie said, very quietly: 'Do you think every mother feels terrified of some maniac *assaulting* her child?'

What did I answer? Possibly I said I didn't know, or that such a terror could hardly be thought unreasonable. But she had gone on, her hand worrying at the swing-chain. 'I do have nightmares about it. I watch her like a hawk all the time. I mean . . . it is . . . the most horrible thing in the world today, don't you think?'

I remember then the intensity of her fear forced me to consider it; I couldn't think of it in such dramatic terms as she did; there seemed to me then, and now, much worse evils which possibly we perform *en masse*, rather than that individual hell which such a man must carry with him all his life. The fact that I couldn't completely agree with her made her worry at this morbid fear. 'Is it because . . . ?' she said. 'No. . . . Nothing ever happened to me, thank God, but maybe my parents were odd about it. Always full of dour warnings about strangers. I never mention it to Lucy. I won't. I think that's bad, don't you? Because I remember how they used to go on about it so.' Then she frowned. 'I can't even pin it down. All I remember once was . . . a kind of unhappy shock that hung about them.'

She never mentioned it again; it was as if she had shown me some disfigurement, a blemish on her nakedness, that she was ashamed of and had in future always to disguise. 'I watch her like a hawk all the time.' Why wasn't Josie with the child that particular afternoon? Rod had said they were quarrelling. Was that the only reason? Was it guilt or desolation that made her commit suicide?

I remember another time in the room behind the antique shop. Lucy was in the yard at the back, playing with a friend on an old Victorian rocking-horse. Josie stood at the window looking out at them. 'Mother says that Lucy is so like me at that age.'

'Were you as mischievous?'

Josie poured out some tea. 'I've no idea. I can't remember much before I was about eight. I can remember that ghastly school at Lewes, then . . . remember all about that . . . but before,' she shrugged, then suddenly she looked quite happy and free. 'Oh yes, I know what I remember, terribly clearly . . . your uncle.'

'So do I. Wish I could forget him.'

Josie looked surprised. 'Oh, do you? But he was wonderful . . . so good with children. He'd buy tiny presents and . . . play with me . . . not a bit like a grown-up, very gentle. I really hated Aunt Janet when she left him, because that meant I'd never see him again.'

'God, you astonish me. I lived with him in that bloody house for ten years, and he never showed me an ounce of affection, and very little kindness. Obviously I lacked your charm.'

Josie laughed and tossed her light brown hair; she wore it drawn back in a pony-tail, a style that only served to elongate her face, magnifying the indrawn look she had. 'Isn't that odd? Because I really do remember him with such happiness.'

I can't face going back to that house. I won't damn well go back to that house. I'll bloody well walk until I drop. I want none of them. I never want to hear their sordid treacherous dramas . . . anyway, for God's sake, Woody has something of the old girl's lying fantasies in him. Maybe that story about him picking the flowers was all lies? But . . . no, it sounded like her. But what the hell am I to do with Rod? I need him. No, that can't be true . . . but why then am I so sunk in misery now, tortured by the fact that he'll be looking for me? Walk up and down the Palace Pier, freak shows and holiday-makers wrapped up against the wind and the salt spray. Call at the junk shop, nod briefly at Miss Curtis, who has the look of Wilkes on her, but none of the heart.

'No, he hasn't been in, Miss Willoughby. I was just closing up.'

'Sold anything?'

She laughs quite gaily. 'Well as a matter of fact, it wasn't a bad afternoon at all. It's the clothes they want . . . the kind my mother used to wear.' She pauses. 'The students you know.'

I think of those trunk-loads back at the house, or did Woody burn all those? I look down and see the dancing shoes. 'Why don't you get rid of those? Burn them.'

She nods sadly. 'Yes. But I think . . . if I did . . . well, it would be like losing her all over again.'

'Oh, he's tougher than that,' I say as I leave.

Back to those damned bars. More bloody freak shows. The Star and Garter's half empty. I walk down across the beach. I can hear the jukebox blaring from the Beach Bar. I think of those women's faces, tense and sharp like little malevolent birds. The clouds are dense and black, and all the lights of the town look extravagantly lurid, like a display of boiled sweets. The piss stench of the public loos merges with frying onions, the plastic windmills whirl in the wind beneath beribboned straw hats that rustle together like dead twigs. I stand there, at the door of the bar, watching them all, I can't see him. I wander through, hating the feel of them as I push and weave through the mass. I feel as if pressed tightly against a gargantuan distortion, but I am part of this freak element; it is as if they all violate me, and I demand it of them. But it's all absurd. I want Rod. Yes, just him, with his balding hair, his dry scaly skin, his tight little muscular body that is hard as if the nerves beneath his flesh have been wound up, coiled as tight as they can extend themselves, so that our love . . . no, not that word . . . our need, for the other explodes. Always . . . a galvanic outburst . . . a tumult of the senses suddenly erupts from the deadness we were oppressed with before.

Trigger amuses me. What does she want from me? She follows me, her body encased in the black leather as dense as the shadows on the beach, her head in its paleness seems disembodied. We talk. I feel suddenly an urgency in her to destroy. What? Whom? A mad idea takes over my mind. If only I could suggest to her that she might break into the house. Yes . . . that's it . . . I want her to. That's what she must destroy. I'd like her to steal everything. To break up the furniture, to plunder that hideous past . . . to set fire to the house, to burn it down. Instead, I give her money, leave her, continue to search for that man.

'What happened? What the hell happened?' Rod was lying in his own blood and vomit, one arm crumpled beneath him; he stared up at me hazily as I bent down and tried to help him to his feet.

'Christ knows.' He swayed unsteadily, then focused, saw it was me. 'Oh, thank God.' He held me tightly to him, his lips, smeared with dried blood, touched my face. I dragged him to the only wash basin; a sailor came in, ignored us both and peed. I slopped some water on to Rod's face.

'Lulu told me you were here. She said you'd got into a fight. For God's sake, what about?'

He shook his head, shaking the drops of water away, then clung on to me again; he sobbed like a child. 'Oh God, let's get out of here.'

A taxi took us up to the hospital. They bound his ribs up, wiped the blood from the wound below his eye; his face was puffed up, beginning to be blotchy with bruising; he looked so bewildered and lost. We went back to the junk shop. He clung to me, half resting his weight on my arm as I took him through the shop and into the room at the back. He groaned and lay down on the mattress. He stank of vomit, drink and disinfectant.

'Christ, they bloody well hate me in there. . . .'

'Why? Why?'

'One of them knows,' he suddenly cried out, locking his fingers together and shaking them.

'Who knows? Which one?'

'I just bloody well sense it . . . they know and they don't want me to know.'

'That's absurd. You damn well know that they hate child-killers more than we do.'

He turned his battered face towards me. I suddenly saw Wilkes again, lying twisted in the grass and nettles. 'Then why was I beaten up on purpose? Two of those sailors were mucking around with Sadie – Trigger's girl – they made out I wanted her. Oh God, I don't know how it started, but when I left the bar, they were outside waiting, both of them. . . .'

'Drunk, that's all. . . .'

'No. I felt them all in there, hating me, as if my pain had suddenly made them feel a terrible guilt, shame, remorse . . . I don't damn well know, but they turned on me. They did, I'm telling you.'

I put a blanket over him, made soothing noises, but he drew me down near him; he was quivering like a trapped rabbit. 'Make love to me,' he said quietly, 'to me, make love. . . .'

His poor bruised body was so helpless beneath my hands. His kisses so desperately hungry. Then when it was over he whimpered.

'What? What is it?'

He didn't speak for a time, then suddenly he said: 'I was wondering . . . did Lucy feel that, when she was dying? Did she feel after the howling panic, when she was bruised and torn with pain, did she feel, as well, at last that she was also cradled with love . . . and . . .' but he was sobbing, 'yes, yes . . . and infinite gentleness?'

Rod

The white venetian blind was slanted against the rays of the sun, so that the whiteness of Emma's room was dappled, colourless shades, muted like worn ivory keys of an old piano. There was something somnolent in the air, in the lazy way she moved from chair to bed, her voice, quite soft, yet exact, nothing drowsy in the way she spoke, and yet I could not find in me any excitement, any curiosity.

'. . . that's not all. The other day I saw what Sadie was wearing. I recognized the rings on her fingers. They used to belong to Saffron.'

I sighed, tried to rouse myself. 'But . . . why are you telling me all this now?'

She closed her eyes. 'I wanted to think about it all carefully. It just . . . well none of it fits together. Woody said he'd fallen down the stairs and hit his head. Maybe he did. But I'm sure Trigger broke into the house. He must have been terrified. Why won't he say? Why didn't Trigger take the odd bits of money that were lying around? I know . . . I just felt it . . . when I came back two days later . . . that the house had been ransacked, and yet it was all very tidy. The money over there,' she pointed, 'was stacked neatly in a pile. All my things in the drawers weren't in the mess I always leave them.'

She frowned and bit her underlip. 'Then I searched for some old clothes . . . Miss Curtis says she can always sell them. Saffron had a vast wardrobe and kept everything. She would have Wilkes get all her favourite clothes out and she'd sit among them, just feeling them, for hours, dreaming about her sordid past. Woody had told me he'd burnt the lot, but you never know whether to believe him or not. So I went upstairs to the attic . . . for if there was anything left that's where it would be. There used to be trunk-loads of the stuff there.' She paused, still frowning.

'Well?'

'The skylight was shattered, but so was everything else, as if some crazed maniac had taken an axe to all Saffron's old dummies

. . . all the clothes were in shreds . . . I mean quite small shreds; not just ripped, but as if a whole host of rats had chewed and spat everything out. The floor is knee-deep in old cloth, and the dummies lie there, in a sea of coloured froth, their huge Edwardian chests carved up.'

'Maybe it's been like that for years? Maybe when he burnt everything else he took an axe to that lot?'

'Perhaps . . . but it didn't seem like that. It looked all newly churned up . . . there wasn't a thick layer of dust over everything . . . and there always used to be.'

'Have you asked him?'

'Yes, of course . . . but, oh God, he looks so ill. Ever since I struck him . . . I think now he will die. I've tried to be as gentle as possible, but now he's got this nervous thing, and whenever you ask him anything, he jumps out of his skin and twitches. . . . He looks so old and broken. But he goes out, you see. That's the other thing . . . every week now, he goes out for a few hours.'

'Where?'

'I don't know. I would have followed him, but though it's always a Friday, it's not always the same time, and . . . Oh, it just seems so ugly.' She got up from the cane rocking-chair. 'No, I don't want to ask him anything, not any more. But . . . I want us both to talk to Trigger.'

'That's easy enough, but she won't tell us anything she doesn't want to.'

'Not at the bar, find out where she lives.'

'Look, surely, if she took nothing of importance, then why the hell are we bothering . . . ?'

'She did, I know. Whatever she took must have been very important.'

'What? What was it?'

She sighed with impatience. 'Oh Roddy, I don't know . . . that's what I must find out.'

What an absurd thing you are, I thought. She loathed so much this museum of her life, and yet now when she had some strange apprehension that something had been taken from it, she was acting like a blind creature, sensitively feeling all the known objects to try and find which detail had vanished.

'Go on ringing the bell,' Emma said.

We were in Waterloo Street, opposite the church. I'd got Trigger's address from one of the girls, making out that I'd got a special job for them both to do. We heard a window being raised. Third floor front, large bay. Sadie hung out of it, shouting down: 'Wha' the 'ell do you want?'

'Can we come up?'

'No,' she said, and yanked the window down again.

'Well, that's certainly to the point,' Emma murmured, then we heard the window go up again.

'I said what you want,' Sadie shouted, pinning her hair back behind her.

'How can we talk down here?' Emma shouted back.

'Okay, okay, wait a minute.' The window came down again and we waited, nearer five minutes than one, before she reappeared. She looked at us both and sniffed. 'We only took this place last week, and we got the decorators in the lounge, see. So I don't know whether I can ask you up.'

'Oh, I'm sorry about that,' Emma murmured. 'Isn't Trigger in?'

'No, she's not. Besides, she's particular about 'oo comes up an' sees us, anyway.' Sadie paused, pushing a strand of hair behind her ear. 'What you want, then?'

'It was purely a friendly call,' I said quickly, trying to smile warmly.

'Oh yes?' she said, one hand involuntarily going upon her hip.

'Not quite,' Emma added sharply. 'You see, Sadie, Beth told us that you both do exhibitions. . . .'

'For Christ's sake,' Sadie cut in, 'don't let Trigger know, she'd murder me.' Then she gave a tiny seductive movement of her body. 'Yeah, that's true, but Beth don't 'ave no right to tell everyone.'

'Only because I asked her,' Emma quickly said.

Sadie looked from one of us to the other. 'When you want it put on then?'

'No, it's not for us . . . it's for . . . friends. Look, Sadie, that's what I want to explain . . . they're awful kinky, and I don't know whether. . . .'

Sadie laughed. 'Cor, there's nothin' I 'aven't done, darlin'. . . .'

She was barely nineteen, I thought, nothing but a kid, with her painted doll's face. Does she really luxuriate in this world of hers? She smiled and nodded to us. 'Okay, come upstairs, but you'll 'ave to put up with the kitchen.'

We followed her up the green and cream stairway over the worn strip of carpet and stepped through a door into a tiny hall. Sadie stood there and looked around her, asking us to admire it. 'They done this first, see? Looks good, don't it?' We agreed fervently that the padded crimson diamond wallpaper with gold stars was perfect. Then she took us into the kitchen, and without asking, poured out three gin-and-limes into small decorated glasses. 'Okay, then, what are these two? Both fellas?'

Emma shook her head.

'What? A man an' a woman? What's up with her then? Is she dykey?'

'How much d'you charge, Sadie?' I asked.

'Depends,' she shrugged. 'All depends what they want. Beth an' I have a straight fee, a tenner each, but if they want anythin' special like, well they 'ave to pay for it, don't they?' We both agreed that this was very reasonable. 'So what they want, then?'

Emma seemed at a loss; she was standing in the kitchen doorway, peering through into the bedroom where the door was just ajar.

'Flogging,' I suggested emphatically.

'We don't do that. Beth don't like it.' She stared at me blankly, her light blue eyes ringed thickly with black; the large false eyelashes fluttered, suggesting perhaps at times she did feel vaguely trapped. 'But we do boots and chains. Beth don't mind bein' chained, says it makes 'er feel like Maid Marion.'

Emma looked interested. 'I never knew she was chained up.'

'Course she was,' Sadie said with outrage, 'by one of 'em kings.' She laughed. 'They were a kinky lot, all right. That's what makes me mad. They look down on us, but what about the Royal Family?'

We both agreed that it was very unjust, and that the Royal Family probably had a huge vault below Buckingham Palace crammed with instruments of torture and sexual deviation that would have gladdened the heart of the Marquis himself. Then Sadie glanced at her minute wrist watch. 'Blimey, I've gotta move.' Then she proudly showed us the watch. 'Present from Trigger, super isn't it? Got real class, Trigger says.' We both examined it and admired it. It was far from cheap. Sadie went into the bedroom; we followed her. She opened a wardrobe that glittered with clothes and picked out a red dress. I saw Emma stare into the wardrobe; a slight frown crossed her face. Sadie held the dress in front of her and looked into the mirror. 'Like it?' she said. 'It's my sexiest,' and she grinned and wriggled her bottom. She had, I must admit, a strange charm; underneath all that sexual knowhow was a sublime naïvety. Besides she was right, she was sexy. I liked it. She undressed calmly in front of us, down to her bra and minute scarlet knickers which were transparent.

'So. When you want us to give this exhibition, then?' She brushed her hair. Emma sidled towards the wardrobe.

'What a lot of gorgeous clothes you've got, Sadie. May I look?'

'Yeah, help yourself.' She sighed. 'I just love clothes. Yeah, I really live for clothes. An' Trigger, she likes me to look sumpthin'. She says next month she'll buy me a fur.' She turned round and looked at us both. 'A real fur, maybe mink . . . tho' I'd love leopard.' She sighed again. 'Think of that. Then I'd be as good as La Lollo. Wouldn't I be?'

'Just as good,' I said. 'In fact better.'

'Would I be, really?'

'Yes, you're better-looking.'

''Ere, do you think so?' and she swivelled round and stared at herself closely in the mirror. She smiled at her reflection, then with a nail, scraped a piece of lipstick off one of her teeth. Emma was still rummaging in the wardrobe and had pulled a suitcase from the back towards the front. She took a quick look at Sadie, then bent down and tried to undo the crocodile straps.

'You 'aven't told me yet, when you want us to do this exhibition.'

'Oh, in the next few days.'

'Can't manage them,' she said with an edge of a haughty booking-clerk. 'Far too busy, 'ave to be over the weekend. What abart Sunday evenin'?'

'Oh I'm sure that will . . .'

Then we heard Trigger's key in the door. Sadie spun round, her finger to her lips, then saw Emma now on her knees, having only managed to undo one strap. ''Ere, what you doin'?' Sadie said, shutting both the wardrobe doors quickly as Trigger came into the room and looked suspiciously at all three of us.

'So we got guests, then, 'ave we, Sadie?'

'Yeah, that's right, darl, they 'eard about our new place, didn't you?' Trigger crossed the room, clutched Sadie's hair at the back and wrenched her head round, then kissed her hard on the lips. Sadie broke away. ''Scuse me, Trigger, but I got to go out now.'

'Why you still workin'? You know you don't 'ave to work now.'

'I like workin', that's why. Cor, I've got to do somethin', 'aven't I?' She gave a little petulant sniff and started to fill her handbag with make-up from the dressing-table.

Trigger leant against the wall and lit a cheroot. ''Aven't seen you two round lately.'

Emma looked tense. She suddenly said: 'Trigger, I know that six weeks ago you broke into the house. I don't blame you. It doesn't really matter. In fact, I even, in an odd way, wanted you to. . . .'

Trigger just smiled, blowing out the smoke slowly; maybe she was aping Bogart or one of those myths.

'. . . but my uncle is ill and frightened. I don't know why.'

'Shart up,' Trigger spat. ''Ere, Sadie, get out.'

Sadie seemed more than ready to; in fact she was half in flight already. She stood at the door, looked back at us and smiled nervously. 'I never know nuthin' of what Trigger does . . . nuthin'.'

'Get out,' she shouted and followed Sadie into the hall, slamming the front door behind her.

'What the hell are you saying?' I whispered. 'For God's sake, be careful.'

We heard Trigger open another door. 'Cor, wha' a bleedin' mess,' she muttered. 'Those decorators are as slow as fuckin' tortoises.' She came back into the bedroom. ''Ere, want a drink then?'

'What the hell did you take?' Emma said.

'Nuthin'. Nuthin' worth takin' was there?'

Emma was pleading with her. 'You got in through the skylight, then what happened? You saw my uncle?'

'What does 'e say, then?'

Emma suddenly flung the wardrobe door open and yanked out the red plush suitcase. She threw it on to the floor. 'You took that. What's in it?'

I saw that for the first time Trigger was afraid. 'That's none of your business.'

'Open it,' Emma said. 'Prove to me that it's none of my business.'

Trigger strode over, picked the suitcase up. 'Feel it, it's light, isn't it? Well then, it's empty, isn't it?' She dropped the suitcase on to the floor, then kicked it under the bed.

'Can we have it back then?' I asked.

She glowered at me. 'Sadie's kind of fond of it. Okay, I took them jewels an' things. I 'ad to 'ave somethin' to put 'em in, didn't I?'

Emma crouched down and pulled it from under the bed. 'I want to see inside it, Trigger.' I was staring at Emma, but I heard the click of the knife, looked up and saw Trigger holding it in her hand.

'Leave it alone, or I'll carve yer up,' she said coldly, staring down at Emma, who glanced up once, then started to fiddle with the other strap.

'You 'eard,' Trigger shrieked, and kicked the suitcase away, bringing the knife down near Emma's cheek.

'For God's sake,' I shouted at the same time, and pulled Emma away. The myth required me to kick the knife out of Trigger's hand and to knock her senseless, but I was a physical coward and loathed all violence. 'Come on, let's go,' I hugged Emma to me.

'Okay, Trigger, then we'll call the police,' Emma said with surprising coolness.

'You'll be bleedin' sorry if you do that. I warn yer.' She went on shouting at us, as we went down the stairs.

The policeman behind the desk looked up coldly, then nodded at us. 'Oh, it's you, Mr. Johnson.' He glanced briefly at Emma, 'The Inspector's not in.' He looked down again at the desk and began to write. 'But he did want to see you about something. Care to wait?'

'How long will he be?'

'Can't tell you.' He looked up and surveyed us both. 'Why don't you go home? Then he'll contact you.' I looked at him; the chill was even more set; it gave him an air of pained martyrdom.

'Why don't you tell him?' Emma whispered, clinging on to my arm. She had lost her sense of command; in these alien surroundings she looked very fragile and entirely lost.

'We want to report a burglary,' I said rather pompously, relieved at last to have something definite to state.

'Oh yes, where?' He became officialdom incarnate immediately. We gave him the address, which he wrote down.

'And when did this happen?'

'Six weeks ago,' Emma said.

He looked at us sadly. 'You mean, you only just noticed?'

'Oh no,' Emma said brightly. 'I knew at once. It was just . . . I didn't think it was important.'

'But you do now?'

Emma nodded. The policeman gave a snort of protest. 'What was taken?'

'A suitcase,' she answered at once, and gave him a detailed and vivid description of it. He wrote it all down.

'And what was in the suitcase?'

She paused. 'I don't know.'

He leant back on his stool and stared at us both again, then he shook his head and tut-tutted. I felt we were both back at school again and what fools we were making of ourselves. We couldn't communicate the urgency Emma felt; so briefly I told him what had happened that afternoon. He brightened up considerably when I mentioned that we had both been threatened with a flick-knife, scribbled away busily, then surveyed us yet again.

He shook his head. 'What I don't understand is, why you're both so thick with this lot of scum. If you ask me you deserve what you get.'

We walked outside into The Lanes. 'Helpful, aren't they?' Emma murmured. 'D'you think they'll search Trigger's place now?'

'God knows.' Then I stopped. 'What the hell does Jones want to see me about? They must have. . . .' Then I hurried on through the The Lanes back to the shop.

'Oh, yes,' Miss Curtis said, looking more flustered than ever. 'He's been here twice. Looking for you, well . . . for you both really.'

'Both?' Emma queried.

'Yes, that's right, because he said he'd been to the house and received no answer. . . .'

'Woody wouldn't open the door to anyone. Thinks they're all gypsies,' she said sourly.

'He seemed most anxious to see you.' She looked away from me, as if embarrassed. 'And Miss Willoughby too.' Then I noticed that the dancing shoes had gone.

'What the hell?'

'Oh dear . . . it really wasn't my fault, Mr. Johnson. . . .'

'Where are they?'

'Sold,' she managed to say as her arms floundered in apology.

'But they were labelled "Not for Sale".'

'Yes, yes, I know . . . but the label was so old, and . . . well, Mrs. Wainwright never noticed.'

'Oh, that's it . . . you were shopping, I suppose. . . .'

'Oh for heaven's sake, Rod, what does it matter?'

We were all talking at once. 'Time and time again I've said when you leave the shop, close it.'

'Yes, I know you have. But I always look after Mrs. Wainwright's shop when she leaves it for a while, and we have been doing better lately. I didn't want to miss the trade.'

'Stop being beastly, Rod, for God's sake.'

'Who bought them?'

'A man, I believe. He paid five shillings.'

Five bloody shillings, I thought. I crossed the road and went into smartiboots with her blue-rinsed hair and her bastardized mock-up four-posters and leather chairs as tightly buttoned as her mouth and arse. 'Who bought them? The dancing shoes?' I shouted.

She placed a bookleaf into a copy of *Antique Fair* and slowly looked up at me in astonishment. 'I beg your pardon?' I repeated the question. 'I'm sorry, Mr. Johnson, but I'm not used to being shouted at.'

Emma had followed me in, and was tugging at my sleeve, trying to get me out of the shop. How absurd it was. Why the hell did it matter to me? I felt the same desperation as Emma had about the contents of the suitcase. Why the hell were we in such a frenzy? I made an effort to calm down. 'I apologize. It's just . . . that it may be . . . just possibly, important.' She didn't smile, but showed her teeth, pushing her tongue momentarily between them; they were all thin and crooked like half-sucked cough lozenges.

She shrugged. 'A rather rough gentleman. . . .'

'Old, thin, fat?'

'No, not at all . . . just rather middle-aged, quite ordinary . . . a rather common accent. I'm sorry, Mr. Johnson, if . . .'

'What did he say? Didn't you think it odd that he wanted a pair of second-hand dancing shoes?'

'Good heavens no. He said he thought they'd fit his daughter.' She paused. 'He didn't seem to me to be the kind of gentleman who would want to afford the cost of a new pair.'

'Would you recognize him again?'

'I should imagine so.'

I crossed back to the junk shop, told Miss Curtis to go, then slunk back onto that dirty mattress. My God, my head ached. I lay there, picturing those shoes . . . part of a collection? Or just encasing the feet of some other pirouetting girl? But I must have fallen asleep. I woke up, saw Emma reading a book in the light of a table lamp, its base sculpted into the form of Pan. How ludicrous that piece of Edwardian folly was, blowing his three pipes and his horns sprouting electric light bulbs. Emma looked up at me: 'We'd better go back to the police station and wait for Jones there.'

We walked back. It was beginning to rain, a light drizzle coming in from the sea. 'You go in,' I said. 'Tell them we'll be in the Star and Garter.'

I didn't wait for her to come out. I wanted several large whiskies inside me. I didn't even care much when she failed to join me. I was trying to understand why the sale of the shoes mattered so damn much. We didn't even know if the killer had a shoe fetish anyway. There were tons of second-hand clothes-shops in that area, all doing good trade, so why shouldn't the sale have been quite innocent? Maybe I just cared because it was another part of Lucy gone, which would never be returned. Sod it, sod them all.

Emma

'Ah, hallo Miss.' I thought Jones looked rather genial. Big, broad, with a handshake like a dog dancing up and down on your palm. He looked as if he could play Father Christmas any time. 'Mr. Johnson's at his favourite sport,' he said laughing. 'Well, I don't mind a good few pints myself sometimes.' He grinned and nodded to the chair. I thought maybe he was overdoing the bluff heartiness.

'Actually it's all to the good. I wanted a few words with you alone. Now,' he sat down behind his desk, 'what can you tell me about your uncle?'

'My uncle? Well . . . what's he done?'

He leant over the desk towards me. 'Look, Miss, I don't want to worry you, but I think maybe he's in a spot of trouble, and we'd like to help. Now, have you noticed him acting strangely lately?'

'He's always been strange.' Why did they always make one feel on the offensive?

Jones looked interested. 'Oh? In what way?'

'I don't think I can explain . . . not quickly.'

'Take your time,' he said, leaning back in the chair. Were they conscious of their clichés, I wondered?

'I daresay he's no stranger than anyone else,' I said sharply. 'Perhaps, it might help me if you could tell me what . . . this *spot* of trouble is.'

He picked up a biro and tapped it on the desk. 'Naturally. I was coming to that.' He looked away out of the window, still tapping. 'We've had our eye on a young lady; as you know, by calling her that I'm being polite. I've seen your report by the way, and we've already searched the place. . . .'

'Did you find the suitcase?'

He bent down and placed it on the desk. 'You mean this one?'

I nodded. 'That's the one. What's in it?'

He opened it. 'Nothing, as you see.'

'But I don't understand, why should she have had that reaction?'

'Because when you were there, there was something in it.

When you left, she panicked, taking whatever it was.' He bent down and smelt the inside. 'Lavender,' he murmured. 'Mmmm, lavender and mothballs. Don't worry, we'll have it properly tested now you've identified it. Daresay we'll know what it contained before the night is out.'

I sat there and felt quite impressed. I warmed to Jones. How efficient the British Police Force was, and how paternal too.

'We'll pick her up, too. Haul her in for questioning. They soon talk. Now look, what you're wondering about. . . .'

'She's been blackmailing him?'

'Quick girl. Or did you know it for certain?'

'It never crossed my mind before that moment.'

'Sure?'

I nodded. He grunted and began tapping the biro again. 'Why? Any ideas?'

'No. It sounds quite wild. Except, well . . . there was that . . .'

'The murder. Miss Wilkes, you mean. I know. We've gone all through the reports last week. Trotter confessed and was hanged. D'you think . . . ?'

I closed my eyes. Oh God, anything now seemed possible. 'Let's suppose that Trigger broke in, ransacked the house, and found some evidence that he'd done in the spinster. . . .'

'But what evidence?'

'A diary, a written confession maybe . . . ?'

'Well, she'd hardly need a suitcase to take that away.'

Jones looked rather pained. 'It isn't a very large case, Miss, and besides, she took some costume jewellery as well, didn't she?'

'True. But I wouldn't think Trigger reads.'

'She's as bright as they're made, that one. . . .'

'But how do you know she's blackmailing him?'

'They meet on Fridays, at the Aquarium. Nice and dark in there.'

'Meet?' The thought of Woody and Trigger having a conversation was very extraordinary.

'Well, they pass close, close enough for him to give her some cash. How much we don't know. I haven't wanted to frighten her off. But your report this afternoon made me change my mind.' He stared at me, then rubbed his chin. 'Could it be anything else? Have a think.'

I sighed. I felt so exhausted and stunned that my mind refused to stir.

'We've been through the Town Hall records. Married he was for a short time.'

'Yes, that's right.'

'D'you know the reason for divorce?'

'No.'

'The wife filed a case: marriage unconsummated.'

'Oh. That doesn't surprise me.'

'Really?' He looked interested again. 'Now why, Miss? Why should you have such a natural reaction to that piece of news?'

Were all Detective Inspectors amateur psychologists I wondered? 'Well, if you once met my uncle, it wouldn't surprise you either.'

'Then that's exactly what I'd better do.' He got up.

'Now?'

'Yes.' He buttoned up his jacket.

'He's a mass of nerves now. He's frightened of everything. . . . You will be very careful?'

'Of course, Miss. I'll drive you back to the house. You can be there.'

'I thought you wanted to talk to Rod?'

'Well, no, not exactly. I just knew that you two were around these days, so I planned . . . to explore the matter. That's all Miss.'

He stopped the car outside the Star and Garter, but Rod wasn't there. Jones turned the car and we drove up North Street, back towards the house. My thoughts were in fragments, sitting there next to him, with the rain now a downpour, slashing against the windscreen. I tried to get some clarity into all the confusion. No, the odd thing was that I found there was no real astonishment, that whatever Woody and Trigger were at, seemed to be part of everything that had gone on before; even Sadie seemed to be an obscene echo of Saffron's youthful stage career; and she, the present Sadie, I felt certain would similarly grow and monstrously decay. But if Trigger was punishing him – and I knew she was, because his manner now was so deeply oppressed – how had she got this power? Jones' theory of some written confession seemed unlikely. Trigger was not the kind of person to have sat down and read a journal as she ransacked a desk.

We reached the house. I ran across the drive in the pouring rain, then let him in. 'Say I'm just a friend,' Jones said.

'But you don't . . . I mean . . . .' How ludicrous he was being, anything less like a friend I couldn't imagine.

'What?'

'Never mind. Look, there's another thing. He locks himself in his room, he always has, and no one ever is allowed inside it except himself.'

Jones nodded grimly, as if this was just what he would expect.

'He may even have gone to bed now.'

'You might not believe it, Miss, but I have quite a doctor's bed-side manner if necessary.' Then we both heard him calling my name, querying who it was.

I whispered to Jones: 'Okay, now's your chance to use it.' Then I called: 'It's all right, Uncle, I'm just coming up.' I knocked at the door. 'Woody, are you okay? Can I get you anything?'

We heard him sigh with relief; his voice had got thinner, with-out resonance in it. 'Ah, it is you, Emma.' Then a pause. 'I'm all right, thank you.'

'Have you eaten anything today?' No answer. 'Woody, unlock the door, I want to see you.' He still didn't reply. 'Come on now, don't be silly. I've got a friend with me. . . .' I looked at Jones with desperation. 'He'd love to . . . meet you.'

'Is it Rod?' he said eagerly.

'No, another friend.'

'What's his name?'

'A Mr. Jones.' There was another long pause, and I tapped on the door again. 'Please, Woody, open the door.'

'I don't want to meet anyone,' he said quietly. 'Please . . . tell them to go away.'

I looked at Jones and shrugged. He murmured: 'Sorry, Miss,' then he banged on the door loudly. 'Look, Mr. Willoughby, I'm here to help you. Now come on, open the door.' We waited. 'What are you frightened of then?'

We heard that thin voice again: 'Help me? Who are you?'

'I could be a friend, if you'd let me.'

'Go away. Emma, take him away.'

I drew Jones into my room and shut the door. I was surprised that he came; I half-expected him to throw his weight at Woody's door and break it open. 'In the morning, does he come out then?'

'Yes.'

'What time?'

'Early . . . he's up around seven.'

'I'll come back then. Have you got another key? I don't want to frighten him back to his rabbit burrow when the front door bell goes.'

'All right.' I found a key and gave it to him. He left. I went back to my uncle's door. 'It's all right, Woody, no one else here now. Just me.'

I heard him make a snuffling noise, then he said: 'Don't leave the house, Emma, will you?'

Rod

Okay, I wasn't sane any more; I was crawling back into the womb. Pretty filthy it was too, half-womb, half catacomb; but it was the only place I could think of where they wouldn't find me. After all this, after all that endless searching and questioning, I didn't want Jones to tell me what he'd found or who he'd got cringing and whimpering in his cells. So here I was, and it looked as if it had been specially built for a dwarf. Not even where the arch was at its height could I stand upright, this sliver of half-moon space crammed in the stones of the Old Esplanade, the rumble of Kings Road traffic above, packed with rotting sails, broken masts, bits of spars and old fishing tackle. The crescent window was almost opaque with filth, but I rubbed away a small circle and stared through it across the beach. Jumbo slept in a hammock slung from hooks in the ceiling, but all it held now was a brown paper bundle, more shapeless than Jumbo himself. I made a kind of couch from the sails and stretched myself beneath the window, listening to all the different sounds of bars and people, of sea, rain, wind, traffic; I could have been on another planet, feeling displaced from all this wreckage.

A mouse crept from beneath the thick folds of sailcloth, twitched its nose, then flew across some junk, scuttling towards a crumpled paper bag. It stopped and disappeared inside it. Then another appeared from the same place and ran towards a crust of bread, nibbling away in endless greed. I watched them. How fragile they seemed. A drunk was crossing the pebbles, his feet a thundery beat as the stones crackled beneath him; he was singing 'I want her now', but seemed not to know any more words. His voice was big, spluttery and hissing with drink as the 'da di dums' merged with the other sounds and cries. One of my legs had got pins and needles. I moved, watching the mice, sighed, tried to rub life back into the limb. The mice, aware that they were not alone, had frozen, not even the semblance of a nose-twitch now. Odd that people run when struck by fear, while the rest of the animal life freezes until the danger has passed. What would happen if

I solidified my torment so that it became an absolute of carved stone . . . a provincial pietà? Josie might have discovered herself there, recognized the pose she wanted as a memorial, except she panicked and chose extinction. I'd taken the drunk's tune and was softly humming it to myself. The mice scampered away, but didn't hide; they each found a new place a little closer to me, their noses now twitching hectically. I rose, and bending down beneath the arch, tried to get some warmth back into my legs. The mice . . . ah yes, now there were three, then four . . . almost posed, seeming to be quite unafraid of this intruder. My eyes were now accustomed to the dim murkiness of this crammed area, and I noticed that Jumbo was like a magpie; little bags of old food and objects littered the place, were stuffed away into corners. And other things: a peg doll, all its paint and varnish worn away, a necklace of red cut-glass, a circle of brass curtain rings, a large matchbox full of buttons; and, sellotaped to the stone wall, a snapshot of a schoolgirl of about sixteen, all legs and arms, grinning awkwardly beneath a tree. Something in the shape of the tree looked familiar . . . yes, of course, it was *that* garden, and . . . yes, it must be Emma. Emma, just before she was in flight. Emma, preparing for flight. Her pointed face bleached by sunshine, waving her school hat at the camera, as if she wanted to shoo it away. Why the hell did Jumbo have this? How did he get it anyway? I stared at the hammock and pushed it. It swung to and fro, with that lazy motion that seemed to suggest summer afternoons, verdant lawns and the click of croquet mallets. Then I began to untie the brown paper parcel; the coarse string knots were loose, and I did it idly, with little curiosity, and felt only a vague amusement when I discovered nothing but clothes. Except that they were all torn and muddied, and . . . yes, as I took out each dress . . . they were all children's dance frocks . . . four, no, five. The hammock heaved and swung as I threw two of them away. The dim light showed me nothing; desperately I tried to identify some colour or design. Two of them seemed coloured; the other three were once, perhaps, white. I felt them all: one was net, stiffened in places with stains; another felt like silk, with raised embroidery, but limp and crumpled with age; the last, silk too, a double frill at the hem, a tinier frill ending the pouched sleeves. I ran towards the window and crouched there, holding the dress, trying to see it closely. There, yes, there, threaded through the waist, a light blue velvet ribbon. I held the little dress close to my eyes, then buried my face in its folds. The dwarf . . . no, not the dwarf . . . he didn't even drive a car . . . he . . . But this was Lucy's dress, and the others . . . ? Where the hell did he get them? Why? How?

I sat there crumpled in the darkness. The neon pineapple sphere at the bottom of West Street swivelled round and round, and sent its orange glare across the corner of the room every half minute. Then I heard his dislocated shuffle below as he raised his misshapen body up the wooden spiral staircase; and I waited, drawing myself back into the darkness. I heard the creak of the trapdoor as he raised it, climbed through and let it softly down again. He was whistling as he pushed away the flap of sailcloth which disguised his retreat, crept through and murmured: 'Come on then, my little beauties. Come along then.' He whistled again, a short musical phrase of five notes, and as he did so, he took up a candle, lit it, and placed it on top of a packing case. The mice had scampered towards him, and now climbed up his arms and legs, clinging to his shoulders; as they did that he rummaged in his pockets and brought out some pieces of cheese. The creatures remained still, tense and expectant; then he whistled again, and two jumped down to each hand and nibbled the cheese from his palms. When they'd finished he raised the candle up and looked about him. 'Okay, Wally, where are you? What's up with you tonight, then?' He whistled again, the same phrase but louder, adding a musical flourish to the tune. 'Somethin' frightened you, eh? Wally, where you gone? Kept a nice chunk of Danish blue I 'ave for you.' Something stirred near me; a huge old grey rat slunk into the candlelight, then sitting on his haunches, put his front paws up, begging. But Jumbo hadn't seen him. Jumbo was staring down at the hammock and the clothes lying in confusion. He swore, raised the candle up high and swivelled round.

I flung myself at him as he shrieked in fright. The candle fell with a splutter of hot wax, but I had him by the arms as he kicked and struggled, and drew him towards the window.

'Christ, it's you, is it?' He stared up at me, the two whites of his eyes bloodied like coral.

I heard myself say as I shook him: 'Tell me, tell me, the truth, that's what I want.'

And at the same time he was whining: 'No, no, Roddy, don't do it to me, no.'

'I'll fuckin' throttle you d'you hear me?' And I had him by the throat, as thick and bloody corded as an ancient olive tree, as he thrashed and moaned; and then I too shrieked out with pain as I felt something like a knife stuck in my arm, and as I cried out I looked down and saw the rat hanging there, swinging as we struggled. Then all the horrors came together, the violence and secret murders, somehow symbolized in that venomous creature gnawing away at me.

I let Jumbo go, and he rolled away whining as I shrieked to him to get the rat off. I felt such horror that I couldn't even touch it, but began to throw my arm about so as to try and dislodge the foul vermin. For a moment Jumbo watched, enjoying the revenge, then he whistled once more, and the thing let go. I aimed a kick at it but it vanished.

'Rats are better friends to me than men,' Jumbo whispered.

My arm hurt like hell. Jumbo re-lit the candle. My fury had gone. I asked him again for the truth, but meekly now, as if requesting a privilege.

'Someone, I don't know who, brought them up here, told me to hide 'em.'

'Who told you?'

'Someone,' he said glumly.

'You know damn well what they are.'

'No. Just a bunch of old rags.'

'Oh bloody Christ, Jumbo. All I've got to do now is to go to Jones with this,' and I held up Lucy's dress, 'and you'll be put away, locked away, whether you like it or not.'

'Not for the first time.'

'Is that what you want?'

He sniffed a bit. 'I thought you were a friend of mine, Roddy.'

'Hell. I was. I am. But the truth is told between friends. Now, Jumbo, tell me who brought these to you?'

He was silent for a moment, then he said: 'Trigger. This afternoon. She brought them.'

I held the dress in a tight bundle beneath my jacket, hailed a taxi. We got to the house and I found I'd no money, Emma came to the door and paid the driver. I stood in the hall, waiting for her to return, not knowing what the hell I would say to her, how I could begin. But as she closed the front door and looked at me questioningly, I took the dress out from beneath my jacket and held it towards her. She touched it. 'Hers?'

'Yes. Trigger took it and others from here. That's what was in the suitcase.'

'Woody? Oh no. It can't be true, Rod.'

'Why not?'

She went into the drawing-room and lit a cigarette. She turned and then nodded. She looked sick. 'I suppose . . . yes, it could, but, well, all I was thinking was that I lived here for so long. He never touched me. He never looked at me in any way . . . he. . . .' She stopped suddenly. 'What are you going to do now? Why are you here?'

'Just to talk to him, that's all.'

'He won't. How can he?'

'He's never . . . never even known who I was?'

'I suppose not.'

I remembered that moment when I had helped him up the stairs, when he had sobbed like a child and laid his head on my shoulder. How pathetic he was then. How could someone like that commit an action so monstrously evil, not once, but again and again? 'I must understand,' I shouted at her.

She closed her eyes, then nodded. 'Yes, I suppose we all must.' We went out into the hall, then she paused. 'The police know that Trigger's been blackmailing him. They don't know why. Jones is coming back in the morning, early.'

I thought, so maybe all this torture did have a meaning; at least now I can try and find out why it happened before Jones, with all the revenge of society, closes in on him. Emma knocked on his door.

'Uncle, Uncle, are you awake?'

There was a slight pause, then we heard him say: 'Emma? So you're still there. Yes, I'm not in bed yet.'

'Can I see you? Rod's here now.'

We heard him moving in the room. 'Always said you were a good girl, Emma. Yes . . . just a moment.' He unlocked the door, peered at us both, then opened it wide. 'Come in . . . look, you've never seen my theatre. It's time you did.' He closed the door behind us, then pulled the curtains of a toy theatre. 'Puppets, you see,' he said gaily. 'I make them myself.'

Emma looked around the room in panic. 'I can't stay,' she said suddenly.

She flew out of the room, banging the door. 'What a shame,' Uncle Woody murmured. I took the dress out from under my jacket and laid it across the theatre. He looked at it for a moment, and then at me.

'Last summer . . . you killed . . .' but I couldn't go on. I started again. 'Last summer . . . the little . . . girl. She . . .' How could I tell him, how could I get the words out? 'She belonged to me.' He was still bent over, staring at the theatre, half-obscured by the tattered white dress, and then darting glances of bewilderment at me.

I tried again. 'Her name . . . Lucy. Her name . . . I was her father. Do you understand?'

He walked back a few paces, then sat down in a chair. He put his head in his hands. 'Yes, yes, I understand.' Then he looked at me with fear. 'What will you do to me?'

'Tell me why. Just tell me why.'

Woody

'. . . a kind of peace. It was the only way, somehow transformed
. . . yes, but not afterwards. No, no, not then. The accidents, they
weren't planned, oh God, no. After the first happened – that was in
the war – my mother knew, and she made me suffer. Yes. But when
they – that is the accidents. . . .'

'The murders,' the man cried.

'. . . always it was somehow to stop the panic. Not only in them,
but in me too. I had to erase that enormous terror which would
suffocate us both. No, not that only – maybe that too was a small
part – but I could not endure to know that they'd grow up, and
away from the – what was it – the myth, maybe, they embodied
then? Oh God knows. I have tried to understand. Yes, that after . . .
what happened. . . .'

'The sex,' the man cried.

'. . . they were tarnished – not necessarily by what I did . . .
because it never hurt them. Oh no. It was so mild, and, well . . .
I never wanted to . . . do what others did . . . not – d'you understand? – unite in any way, because . . . well, that – oh yes – that,
was never part of what it was. But the fact that they'd grow up and
become like her. . . .'

'Who?'

'. . . Saffron May. No. How can I be sure of that? Perhaps they
did then seem like her, as she might have been, so that . . . my
horror . . . of them growing into the monster of. . . . Please, you
must forgive me. But I too would like to be accurate now, and. . . .'

'Hide nothing.'

'. . . the accidents . . .'

'The killings.'

'Yes. The killings. Were they – I now ask – part of the . . . what
I loved?'

'The sex.'

'Yes. The sex. I think it must have grown, all without my – at the
time – being aware, but . . . it began, so quietly and. . . .'

'Did she suffer?'

'Who?'

'Much, did she suffer much? My daughter? Where did you keep her for three days? Where? Tell me.'

'Here, all of them here.'

'But for three days?'

'Which one? Oh, forgive me, sir, if you shout like this – as you see – it makes me tremble, and . . . well, I can't. Everything goes, vanishes. All that turmoil . . . and – as you see – I want, I need, I will tell you. Be patient . . . please.'

He sat back in the chair. He hadn't looked at me once. He covered his eyes with his fingers and rocked in the chair, back and forwards. 'Patient, yes,' he whispered.

'Go on.'

'Nothing. Just nothing, I can't remember.'

'Think.'

'They were the same, all of them. . . . Does it matter which one it was?'

'You were driving your car,' the man said. 'From your car you would see a child. Then what happened?'

'Searching. I'd be driving the car, searching. Yes. Always because . . . something terrible had gone on and on, for days – no for weeks, months, here. The pressure was intolerable. It drove me back, always into the only way I'd learnt, had known – how, secretly, I could have power again, over her.'

'Who?'

'Always . . . I'd know that I mustn't take that way out, that to do that I'd be hated and reviled, but . . . I was driven into it.'

'How? How? How?' the man shouted.

'. . . driving through those endless streets. Searching. Sweets. Yes, I'd offer them sweets, take them for a little drive. . . . Strange, you know, never frightened they'd be – oh no – you see, I had a way with children – it's the only gift I have – make them at home. I would feel – I know that – they felt quite secure with me. I understood them, you see, loved the way they thought and saw things – so unique – not like older people at all. They saw everything with such freshness, oh it was so good to be with them, to chatter away. . . . Take them, I would, into the Peter Pan place, and we'd be there together . . . well, like brother and sister really. Then, maybe they'd worry a bit, and I'd say that I'd drive them home. So then I did, but it was my home, not theirs – after all that joy, I couldn't bear to lose them. Then I'd show them the theatre, and we'd play with that together again – oh, that always excited them, because I got clever – all sorts of puppets we'd play with. It was a happy time. Oh yes, they'd worry a bit. But, you see – the funny thing is – they trusted me. Oh yes. D'you know something? – they weren't happy children, not before they knew me. . . .'

'What? What?' the man shouted.

'. . . no, not one of them. Frightened to go home, often they were. Not saying they didn't love their mothers and fathers – oh no – not saying that, but, oh . . . I think, maybe, that's how we always recognized each other. They needed me as much as I needed them.'

'Try and say it all again,' the man begged. He took his hands from his eyes and stared at me for the first time, then wrung his hands and echoed quietly: 'You recognized each other.'

'. . . made out I was a doctor – special for children – Doctor Norwood. Then sometimes they'd call me Uncle Norry. Both names were very special. Yes, yes, that's it. . . . sit on my knee. They would tell me all about their Mums and Dads – yes, my God, how I knew it all. How I could tell them that I heard all the quarrels, all the filthy language, all the screaming and shouting, all the tears. Oh yes, we were two spirits close together. . . .'

'Lucy . . . mine. What did she tell you?' the man moaned.

'The names . . . I don't always remember the names . . . forgive me.'

'The last,' he cried.

'Oh my God, she – that was a dreadful mistake. Sir, I'd rather not. . . . I take it she was a close relation?' I looked away from the man's face. I had never seen such naked suffering on a human face before; his torment terrified and appalled me. He was so frozen and still, like a piece of knotted wood roughly carved into the semblance of a medieval Christ. My hunted mind drew back, trying to recall again those joys I had known, so that in communicating them I might make him see the happiness too. 'Yes, sometimes . . . after the games, after the puppet shows . . . they'd worry, and want

to get back home. Frightened, I daresay, of their parents, but – oh
yes – knowing too that they'd be worried. And then maybe they'd
cry a little, and get suddenly – oh – so upset. . . . How that would
tear my heart. I couldn't bear to see their little faces screwed up in
tears and that . . . sudden fear of the unknown. . . .'

'What then?'

How fierce his questions were. They made me stutter. Yet how
relieved I was to be able to tell it, at last to find another human
being who needed to know as much as I needed to tell. 'I'd say I'd
ring their parents, and pretend that I had. Then, sometimes, I'd
say that, as a doctor special for children, we'd agreed – that is the
parents and myself – that she'd stay a few days with me. . . . Yes,
that's what I said.'

'Did they believe you?'

'I'm not sure. Not always perhaps. Sometimes, maybe, they felt
. . . something akin to relief. I'd give them their medicine – always
nice things they had to eat and drink – oh yes – real treats I had for
them, all the time. . . .'

'What medicine?'

'Oh . . . dear me, nothing to harm them. I used to steal Saffron's
sleeping tablets . . . because – well, the very first – oh God – that's
how she knew. She screamed the place down. You see, it was the
first I'd ever brought back here, and I was in a torment, shocked,
so I had to get something to quieten her down.'

'The sleeping tablets.'

'Yes. Had to force them down – struggled and bit me she did –
but . . . that was all for her own good, you see. . . .'

'The first. In the war, you said?'

'That old bitch pretended to have got in touch with her spirit. . . .
Yes. Well, that was the torment, I never knew whether she had or
not. So that all the time I'd hear that name – "Little Jenny Dove
spoke to me this afternoon," Saffron would say. Then give me
orders – oh horrible things she made me do, vile despicable things
. . . "Jenny Dove wishes it," she'd cry. . . .'

'What things?'

I stared at him. Oh dear God, how I remembered all that so
clearly. 'Wilkes would bring up the tea to my mother on a tray –
beautiful china she had, so thin you could see the light through

it. Then Wilkes would leave, and once – oh, more than once it happened – she'd pour herself out a cup of tea. But not me, no, oh no. She made me drink . . . something else.'

'What?'

I spoke the words slowly. I needed the man to understand. 'Her own urine. From the cup, yes. Had to drink, as she watched me. Once, it was still warm from her body. Drink it all down. She said it was my punishment. She said: "The spirit world decreed it." ' I lowered my head and murmured. 'There were other punishments.'

'Why did she never tell the police? Why for God's sake?'

'Oh, she was such a proud woman. And she hated me, you see – always did – for not being a fine handsome gallant man like my father. She loved him – oh yes she did – and the shame, and humiliation, of owning to the world that her own son had committed these . . . dreadful crimes – oh that would have killed her. She was a vulgar, common and cruel woman, who married into a family she believed was – well, she always told me: "The Willoughby family belong to the true aristocracy." She thought we meant something – yes something – in this world. . . .'

'The other punishments . . . what other punishments?'

'Must I tell you?'

'Yes.'

'She made me strip . . . take every stitch of clothing off . . . stand there in her room, as naked as I was born. . . . And then she'd laugh – oh yes – and with her ebony stick . . . she'd prod at my secret parts, prod them and laugh. Because she said they reminded her of a piglet's . . . tail.'

I began to cry at the shame of it all. I couldn't listen to what he was asking, but he began to raise his voice and shout at me again.

'But the punishments never stopped you, did they?'

I took my spectacles off and wiped my eyes, tried to see him in the blur. Yes, he was still sitting in the chair, but leaning forward now towards me. He shouted again.

'No,' I said quietly. 'Emma did.'

'What?'

'That's why it was all so terrible when she ran away. Oh God forgive me. . . .'

'How did Emma stop it?'

'By being here. That's all. By living here, in the same house –
oh, how I blessed her for that – and never a fear she felt for the old
bitch. But I knew she was laughing and ridiculing her – how that
gave me strength – yes, yes, the power to endure her humiliations.
Besides, I knew that Saffron was waiting. Waiting all the time for
me to touch Emma. Maybe, even . . . she hoped that I'd kill her.
Because she was Thomas's child and no part of her – maybe that
was the revenge she sought. So to do nothing, just to exist with
Emma here – though she could not love me, for I did not dare to
show her the . . . affection I felt. . . . No, somehow, in those years I
could begin to control all the broken fragments of my life. But, in
small ways, without her knowing, I could help her.'

I felt happy again, and the pain had gone from the man's face.
'I knew she loved reading, I knew she borrowed books from the
library downstairs, so I hid the money there, which – bless her –
she used. She had a lot of freedom, for I knew this house could
destroy anyone. No, Emma I felt was my little daughter, and that
was my greatest secret.'

'She would have given you back love, if she'd known,' the man
said, for the first time a note of kindness in his voice.

'Ah yes. But then, she would have been . . . in danger.' I closed
my eyes. 'How could I risk that?'

'But when she . . . began to grow up, did the effect she had on
you, did it still work?'

'Oh yes. . . . She got tall very quickly, and thin – always thin she
was – and so bright. Secretly – dear me – how proud I was that she
got on so well at school. Mind you, in those last years she wasn't
much here at all. Head girl she was, won a scholarship to Oxford.
Then, when she found – well, you remember sir, how bad that was
– Wilkes being murdered, and . . . she ran off. I didn't know where.
I travelled up to Oxford the following winter, thinking maybe she
was. . . . No, not there.'

'She went to Paris.'

'So far away? I wonder why?'

'Farther than that, then on to the States . . .'

'Not Oxford? How strange.'

'Oh yes, she got back there too, but not for long. She can't stop
anywhere.'

Silence. Such a strange silence. I stared at the man. I had never thought of him as Emma's lover. I could not think of those things ever, for they disgusted me, and the fact that he was – must be, I supposed – should make him an enemy, a creature for me to despise and resent.

The man was talking softly, leaning forward again, towards me. 'After she ran away, afterwards, when she left this house, what happened then?'

I shook my head. 'I was so confused, oh terribly . . . somehow engulfed by losing her, and the horror of Wilkes lying there. Then, you see, there was just Saffron and myself. Just the two of us together in the house. She wouldn't have a nurse or anyone else to look after her. I did everything. Cleared up every night and day, all the filth. . . . And her humiliations, they never ceased . . . somehow, they became worse, because I never got any peace from her. Maybe you say I should have had the strength to leave her altogether, get a nurse in, or get her into some home. But I never had any will of my own where she was concerned. She induced in me . . . stark terror, yes. But I did leave her . . . I used to leave her for three days at a time, with no food, nothing. But that was only because – well, I had that delight – my own secret companion, hidden in my own room. You see, that was the only way I had the power. . . . Or I. . . . That was it. . . .'

'Bournemouth, you drove to Bournemouth, is that right?'

'Did I?'

'A long way, you must have driven for, say, three hours, maybe a bit less.'

'Yes, I remember now – you're right, sir – yes, you are. . . . She was quite a happy girl, didn't mind the drive, wanted to see the ponies in the New Forest. We walked there for a long time – yes, that was it – then she wanted to go back home, and. . . . I gave her some tea in a place near a river. Lots of boats about – we rode on one, I think. . . . Oh, that was a very happy day. She'd been to a party – yes – and had such a pretty dress on, but – maybe that was the next day we rode on the boat – forgive me. I can't quite recall. . . .'

'Did you bring her back here?'

'No, no, it was too far. When I tried she screamed, and . . . I told her the tablets were sweets, so. . . . No, that one – I'm quite mis-

taken, sir – she never went on a boat, no, it was all an accident. . . .
I left her near the ponies.'

'Dead?'

'Did I? Saffron was dead, when I got back she was dead. So at
last I was free. Oh, can you imagine that – yes – how happy and
triumphant I felt then. She'd had the third stroke. Twisted she was,
dreadful to see, all distorted, like the great spiked root of an old
rotting tree. At long last, after those long tortuous years . . . now
I was alone. . . .'

'To go on killing. What damned image was it? What myth?
Don't you know yet?'

We stared at each other for a while. I shook my head. Nothing
was in any right sequence. He terrified me. At some moments a
look in him of the monstrous anger of God, the great Jehovah;
then when he spoke kindly, I felt – yes – almost . . . infinite mercy.
This man does understand. Yes, I think he does.

'Try and tell me why they were all dressed similarly.'

'Dressed? You mean, the way they . . . danced. Oh yes, that
always had to happen. Dance for me, I'd say. Then I'd pretend to be
an audience in the theatre – oh yes – they all danced so prettily. . . .'

'Why? Why that?'

I shook my head and looked about the room for some reassurance. Surely somewhere in my seclusion there was something
that would help the man. I got up, went to the theatre, and there
behind the scenery I found Jim Crow. 'Bit ragged, he is now,' I said.
'Look, his check trousers are all frayed, and that red jacket used to
have little gold buttons.' I gave him the puppet, and he took it and
stared at it for a while.

'. . . always, when I had them there, sitting on my knee – maybe
I did feel warm and good – as if I was in Florida – or some place
like that – maybe I did. . . .'

'For fuck's sake,' he threw the puppet away. 'Lies, damned lies
. . . tell me the truth, can't you? I've studied you, the anonymous
you for over a year now. I know your habits, the way you did them
in, I know they were all, all. . . .' He turned round, put his head in
his hands and sobbed. Then in a different voice I heard him say: 'At
the autopsy, traces of barbiturates were discovered, and sperma-
tozoa in. . . .'

'. . . not so, that's untrue. Where did you hear it?'

'Facts don't lie. Science can't lie. Police records don't lie.'

'. . . yes, I see. . . . I forget – please sir – don't be angry with me. For what will happen to us all? Just think of that. I beg you. The truth is never simple, never clear, surely?'

'You assaulted them? Yes. Is that what happened to Lucy? How? What happened to her? Oh for God's sake, tell me, then let me rest.'

'. . . it was never intended. Never. Only, after she was dead – when I found Saffron's great corpse and exulted – ah yes – I suppose the . . . freedom I felt then took other forms. I was her son – how could one deny it? – she bred corruption – isn't that so? But, sir – don't you see? – they never saw me, they didn't know, they were fast asleep. . . . I would have done nothing dirty if they'd been awake. It was always . . . best like that, because it was a dream, you see. I never hurt them, never. . . .'

'You murdered them,' he screamed.

'Yes, again and again – I agree with you, sir – I killed them, over and over again, as I loved them all, over and over again.' He stared down at me with those eyes of thunder and disbelief. 'Believe me – how could I distinguish between dying and loving? If I killed them, it was because they were so dear to me – no, that is too simple, too. . . . Oh God, such sweet treasures lying curled in my arms. . . .'

'You choked them to death. You strangled your little treasures.' He shouted again and again at me.

And I was shrieking too, against all he was shouting. 'No. No. NO. Lies. All lies. They went quietly. Like little doves. Their tiny lives . . . fluttered in my hands and faded away.'

He was hunched on the floor, his face again in his hands. 'The last one,' he whispered, 'last summer . . . what happened?'

Then the door opened. Emma stood there. 'Come away,' she said. 'Come away now. You know enough.' Then she walked over to him, bent down and put her arms around him; so entwined they were as one, with him swaying with grief and she whispering words of soft love and murmuring all the time for him to leave me.

Rod

'The last one. Lucy . . . last summer,' I said to the broken shuffling creature in his frayed suit, with the look on his face of existing somewhere else: a shattering despairing world where no other soul would ever reach him.

But Emma went on begging and whimpering, kissing me softly, both our tears salty on our lips. 'Come away, come away, please . . . you *know* now.'

'How the hell can I ever know?' I shouted. 'Not really know.' And I turned back and stared at the old man. 'Last summer, you were in your car?' He shook his head. 'You were walking down Castle Street, down the hill, towards the pavilion . . . ?'

'Buying tickets . . . yes. Yes, the Brahms cello and violin concerto. I wanted to hear it just once more.'

'You saw a small girl, dressed in white and. . . .'

'Don't, don't,' Emma cried.

'A blue velvet ribbon, yes . . . and a blue coat which she had over her arm. Crying – oh, dear me, yes – I remember. . . .'

'She was ringing a front door bell? Yes? At a house in Castle Street?'

The old man shook his head. Emma started to pull me away. I looked at her, and suddenly saw in her pale startled face the tiny terrified girl she must once have been. But something else disturbed her, something she saw in my own face, for she shook her head, closed her eyes for a second, then slowly rose and left the room again.

He stared at the door as it closed, and murmured: 'This little child was sitting on a bench, just the other side of the concert hall – you know, sir – in the Pavilion Gardens. . . .'

'Yes, yes, I know. But crying . . . ?'

'Well, not then. Perhaps not then. . . . I'd bought the ticket – looking forward to the concert the next Sunday, I was – but I too, yes – I was sitting on a seat feeding the pigeons – they were clustered all round me, pecking away, and. . . .'

'The truth,' I begged him. 'Try and remember exactly.' Oh God, the way his mind meandered into these bloody trivialities; yet every shred of information mattered to me, like a faded and ancient script I had to try and decipher.

'. . . of course, I was very conscious of her, sitting there too. . . .'

'. . . the bench, on the same bench?'

'Oh no. Maybe – yes – perhaps, two away – other people between us. I smiled at her and she came over.'

'No. No. You went over to her.'

He lowered his head and frowned. 'I don't . . . believe so. Because . . . I can see her standing there in front of me. And I gave her some bread, and we both fed the birds, and then – oh yes – we went across to the café, and . . . I bought some cake and tea, and – more birds, we kept on feeding birds.' He laughed. 'Oh yes. There was one old floppy fellow of a pigeon that made us laugh so, because – well, he waddled – and she clapped her hands, and thought he was so like. . . .'

'Who?'

'. . . now let me see. Yes, one leg was wounded, so he hopped about – Nonnytoddle, she called him. "We must be kind to Nonny-toddle," she kept on saying. So I bought extra cake, and she picked out the cherries, and gave the birds. . . .'

Lucy's pet name for Josie's father because of his limp. Oh yes, how I could hear now Josie's tight voice saying: 'You must be kind to Nonny, darling.' I looked back at the old man; he was still smiling and nodding his head gently, as if it was wine and roses all the way. 'You said she was crying,' I mentioned again, viciously.

'Oh, afterwards, yes . . . Maybe then . . . after we'd fed the birds, and I said "Now let me take you home." Then, yes – she didn't want to go home. She shook her head and started to cry a little. . . .'

'Damn bloody lies,' I shouted. I wanted to grab the man and shake the truth from him, but he flinched away now, looking at me in fear.

'I tried – oh, believe me – how I tried – I didn't want to take her back. I wanted her to be safe. I had decided – told myself – that she must go home, that I'd take her there. It was all quite clear in my head. But how could I endure her own pain and misery?'

I was trying like hell to keep my voice calm and under control. I said slowly: 'Did she ever . . . did she explain why? Why she didn't want to go home?'

He glanced up at me. 'Oh, the same – always the same . . . frightened, quarrelling, you know. . . .'

We couldn't have failed her. We couldn't have failed her that much? How, if we both loved her so much, more dearly than our own lives, how could she have felt rejected? It just didn't fit in.

'. . . something in particular.' He frowned. 'Ah yes – I couldn't quite understand her.' He stared up at me. 'It was the unicorn.'

I heard myself say: 'Yes?' That word echoed, sending painful and ugly reverberations in my memory. 'What about . . . the unicorn?'

'It distressed her so much,' he answered simply.

An absurd bit of information floated up into my mind. I thought: The horn of this mythical beast was reputed to possess magical or medicinal properties. The man was silent, lost in some other memory that I couldn't yet prise out of him. Then suddenly I knew. That was it. Thank God, yes, Lucy's painting still pinned on her old bedroom wall: The Angel, the Robot and the Unicorn. But why? Why the hell did that have any importance?

He was talking softly: 'Her two little hands were in mine. She said to me: "Daddy in a rage broke it, with his fist, Daddy did, he did."'

'No. What the fuck did she mean?' I was shouting again.

'But I told her – I said that I'd got one at my home . . . oh yes. . . . There it is,' he pointed over to the theatre, '. . . that it was the nicest, jolliest unicorn that ever existed, with a little silver horn and a grey-and-white dappled body, and. . . .'

Yes, then I remembered. Oh what a time ago, what years or centuries. . . . Was she three or four? Why did I never know that that mattered so much to her? It was my present to her one Christmas. It was hanging on the tree, a tiny Victorian egg-cup in the shape of a unicorn. Every morning she had used it. The boiled egg which Josie insisted she ate . . . but which she seldom liked. But always in the unicorn cup, and, yes, hadn't I made up stories about unicorns . . . ? So that she'd eat the egg, and . . . and then, one afternoon – oh the terror of it – the scene in all its bitterness and squalor flooded back into my mind. Josie's nagging and ranting that went on and on, for an hour or more, and I'd lost my temper, for I knew always that violence frightened Josie, and was the only way I could stop that voice biting and gnawing into my soul. I was sitting at the kitchen table, and, yes . . . the egg-cup was the only thing there. I picked it up and smashed it, shouting out at Josie as I did. I smashed it down in my fist and it splintered in my hand and Lucy cried, yes, yes, she cried. . . . But that happened a long time before, maybe a whole year before.

I looked again at the man chattering away about his wretched puppets. Why the hell did he know more about Lucy than I did? That must be the ultimate cruelty. Suddenly I felt a maniac hatred for him, this loathsome creature who dealt in panic and destruction. I wanted to kill him. An immense surge of violence swept over me, and I rose from the chair. But it wasn't him I struck, but the theatre, sweeping it from the table, pulling it to bits, and I shouted as I did so – God knows what – and then stamping on it and kicking the pieces about the room. The door had opened again, and Emma was standing there looking at me and then at the old man, who just looked stunned; he hadn't moved or said a word; he just stared at the coloured bits of cardboard, the tangled strings and absurd dislocated little wooden bodies.

'It's almost dawn,' Emma said quietly.

The man bent down and picked something up from the debris. 'There,' he whispered, 'there it is.' I stared down in the palm of his hand and saw the unicorn. It was quite perfect, its elegant legs bent in the movement of trotting.

'You took her back here? Here? That's what you showed her?'

'Enough, please, enough, enough,' Emma murmured.

'She was very happy,' he said quietly. 'For a time, very happy.'

I spoke the words like a ritual. 'Then she wanted to go home?'

'She wanted to go home.'

'Enough, enough . . . please.'

'So you gave her the tablets.'

'The sweets – yes – and a long warm drink of chocolate, and she went to sleep here. . . .' He pointed to the bed.

'Then . . . what then?'

'Always – yes, always – I undressed them . . . said my prayers for both of us, laid her quietly between the sheets – clean and pressed, straight from the laundry. . . .'

I was a long way away, don't know where, hearing the voice down a long dim tunnel, seeing the man, the room, through the wrong end of a telescope, so that he and everything else was small, distorted, not real at all. My daughter never slept in that bed. This man never killed her. This silly pathetic old creature, he never climbed into the same bed, naked, as she was; he never held her close to him, tight like a hard knot, pressed deep to his withered skin; her flesh never met his; he never murmured those absurd words of love; she never woke up screaming in the middle of the night in a panic of desolation and loss, no, she didn't wake up screaming. . . .

'Not in the middle of the night,' I screamed at him. 'She didn't wake up shrieking, asking for Mummy. Did she? Is that the truth?'

He nodded at me.

'Come away,' Emma said. 'Come away, now . . . please. . . .'

'Killed her,' the man said.

'How?'

'With the pillow . . . I didn't mean – you see – surely you can understand. . . .' His words tumbled over each other in disordered chaos. 'Just wanted to stop her cries – quietly, oh so quietly – I wept so – when I found, when she wasn't. . . . Oh, how I cried so, all that night and morning . . . begging her to come back to me, begging, begging all the time. . . .' He started to cry again.

Emma pulled me away, out of the room. She took me away, down the stairs and through to the kitchen. I sat there. The dawn light softly suffused the tangled garden, making the autumn red leaves as fiery as tongues of flame.

What silence, what immensity of silence, sitting either side of the table, not able to say one word, not knowing any words that could communicate what we knew now, what had swept through us, leaving a gulf, a chasm as wide and deep as everything the human soul has ever clumsily striven for. We looked at each other, made no movement; we sat, waiting . . . but for what? Jones and the bureaucratic revenge of society? How could that touch any one of the three of us? How could the squalor of prison touch the torment he already had?

She glanced at her watch, and at last she spoke: 'What will you do? What is there to do?'

'Nothing. I can do nothing. . . .'

'Are you a better creature now for knowing what you do?' she asked savagely.

'Better? What an odd word. If you said "wiser" I would have laughed. "Better" leaves me puzzled. What, what is it you mean?'

'I could not endure the grotesque masochism, both of you gnawing away at each other. . . .'

'And your part, yours . . . were you as innocent as them?'

'How could I have known,' she said brokenly, 'that I was any help to him? That I could have been more help to him?'

I was conscious of the kitchen clock ticking in the silence.

'What time did Jones say?'

'He'll be here, soon. Oh Rod, how can we let him . . . go through all that? It will kill him.'

'Yes.'

'But what . . . ?' She looked helpless, utterly lost. 'Do you understand anything more?'

'A little more, perhaps.'

'What?'

'That he . . . yes, he perhaps has suffered more than I have.'

'How can that help you?'

'Nor could it help the child. . . .'

'Lucy, she was Lucy, that was her name,' Emma screamed. 'He kept on saying "them", as if they were all the same, as if they were just phantoms from his mind, but they were. . . .'

Then we heard the front door open and the soft sound of someone in the hall. 'Will you tell him?' Emma asked.

'There's nothing . . . nothing any more I can tell.'

'Yesterday I saw a man winding up a bandage,' she said. 'He was standing at a street corner, and so slowly and carefully winding this thin white bandage. And I thought that the bandage was so small, so inadequate, but the concentration on his face was so intense, so passionate.' She looked at me and then at Jones standing in the doorway. 'Why should he have mattered to me so much?'

ALSO AVAILABLE FROM VALANCOURT BOOKS

MICHAEL ARLEN	Hell! said the Duchess
R. C. ASHBY (RUBY FERGUSON)	He Arrived at Dusk
FRANK BAKER	The Birds
WALTER BAXTER	Look Down in Mercy
CHARLES BEAUMONT	The Hunger and Other Stories
DAVID BENEDICTUS	The Fourth of June
PAUL BINDING	Harmonica's Bridegroom
CHARLES BIRKIN	The Smell of Evil
JOHN BLACKBURN	A Scent of New-Mown Hay
	Broken Boy
	Blue Octavo
	A Ring of Roses
	Children of the Night
	The Flame and the Wind
	Nothing but the Night
	Bury Him Darkly
	Our Lady of Pain
	Devil Daddy
	The Household Traitors
	The Face of the Lion
	The Cyclops Goblet
	A Beastly Business
	The Bad Penny
THOMAS BLACKBURN	A Clip of Steel
	The Feast of the Wolf
JOHN BRAINE	Room at the Top
	The Vodi
JACK CADY	The Well
MICHAEL CAMPBELL	Lord Dismiss Us
R. CHETWYND-HAYES	The Monster Club
ISABEL COLEGATE	The Blackmailer
BASIL COPPER	The Great White Space
	Necropolis
HUNTER DAVIES	Body Charge
JENNIFER DAWSON	The Ha-Ha
FRANK DE FELITTA	The Entity
A. E. ELLIS	The Rack
BARRY ENGLAND	Figures in a Landscape
RONALD FRASER	Flower Phantoms